EUSTACE

CATHERINE JINKS was born in Brisbane in 1963 and grew up in Sydney and Papua New Guinea. She studied medieval history at university, and her love of reading led her to become a writer. She lives in the Blue Mountains in New South Wales with her Canadian husband, Peter, and her daughter, Hannah.

Catherine Jinks is the author of over twenty books for children and adults, including the award-winning Pagan series.

EUSTACE

CASE #2

Allie's Ghost Hunters

CATHERINE JINKS

ALLEN&UNWIN

To Fiona Rhodes,
with gratitude

First published in 2003
This edition published in 2007

Allen & Unwin
83 Alexander St
Crows Nest NSW 2065
Australia
Phone: (61 2) 8425 0100
Fax: (61 2) 9906 2218
Email: info@allenandunwin.com
Web: www.allenandunwin.com

National Library of Australia
Cataloguing-in-Publication entry:

Jinks, Catherine, 1963–.
Eustace: a ghost story.

For ages 10–14.
ISBN 9781741146608.

1. Ghosts – Juvenile fiction. 2. Hill End (N.S.W.) – Juvenile fiction. I. Title.
(Series: Jinks, Catherine, 1963– Allie's ghost hunters).

A823.3

Cover design by Tabitha King
Text design by Jo Hunt and Tabitha King
Set in 13 on 15.5pt Weiss by Midland Typesetters
Printed in Australia by McPherson's Printing Group

10 9 8 7 6 5 4 3 2 1

PROLOGUE

Once upon a time, I didn't believe in ghosts. Then my family moved into a haunted house. You may have heard of the ghost who was haunting it; her name was Eglantine, and she's quite famous now. There was a report about her on Channel Nine, and an American program called 'Stranger than Fiction' made an entire episode about her. She's still a hot topic on the Internet, despite the fact that she disappeared more than six months ago.

After she left, I figured that I'd learned just about all there is to know about the paranormal. But what I didn't realise then – and do now – is that dealing with one ghost doesn't make you an expert. There are no real experts when it comes to ghosts. It's not like that movie *Ghostbusters*. As far as I can see, every ghost is different from every other ghost, because every person is different from every other person. That's why research is so important. It's easier to deal with a ghost if you know exactly what ghost you're dealing with.

Not that you're certain to get rid of it, even then. That's what I've discovered. They're tricky things, ghosts; I didn't realise how tricky, before I went to Hill End. I didn't understand that just because you've seen one ghost, it doesn't necessarily mean you've seen them all.

CHAPTER # one

The Hill End trip was a school excursion. A camping trip, to be exact. There were eighteen people on the bus that pulled away from our school one Friday morning: a teacher, five parents (including my mum) and twelve kids (including me). The group might have been bigger if we hadn't been going on a camping trip, but it was probably just as well that no one else wanted to come, because the bowels of the bus were absolutely stuffed with gear. Eskies and tent poles and gym bags and frying pans and I don't know what else. There wasn't room for even one more fire-lighter. You'd have thought that we were colonising Mars, or something. The bus could hardly move up the steeper hills.

Personally, I would have preferred to go by car. But a bus had been hired, so I was stuck in the same vehicle with kids like Amy Driscoll and Malcolm Morling for *four hours*, except when we were let off, at Lithgow and Mudgee, to buy food and go to the toilet. As a matter of fact, I don't really want to talk about that bus trip. You probably don't want to hear about it either, because long-distance school bus trips are all the same: there's always someone who throws up, and someone who spills a drink, and someone who takes his pants down and sticks his bare bum against the back window. This one was no different. By the time we reached Hill End, my mum was beginning to have second thoughts about the whole expedition. She's not used to dealing with masses of kids, you see. She works in a bank, and as an artist's model, and she also does a bit of tarot reading on the side. They're all very *peaceful* jobs. You don't get much yelling or scuffling or flying lollies when you're in artists' studios or bank branches. And even my brother Bethan isn't too bad most of the time. Not like Malcolm Morling.

When we finally chugged down the long, leafy road that leads into Hill End, poor Mum had a throbbing headache. It hadn't been a pleasant journey, what with the bumpy, unsealed road between Mudgee and Hill End, and the boys down the back making faces and rude gestures at people stuck behind us in their cars, and Tammy Ng throwing up into an empty garbage bag. I felt sorry for Tammy; I knew that she would never hear the end of it. I felt sorry for Mum too, because she'd forgotten to pack the Panadol. And I felt very, very sorry for myself, because Jesse Gerangelos had just spent the previous three hours fooling around with Amy Driscoll.

As a matter of fact, I reckon that Amy Driscoll probably signed up for the trip so she could spend the whole weekend flirting with Jesse. She was certainly off to a good start on the bus, despite the fact that her father was there. But her father, whose name is Victor, wasn't especially interested in what Amy was doing. He was too busy flirting with Tammy's mum, who is very pretty. The other parents on the bus were Angus's dad, who is big and hairy and who didn't talk much, and Tony's mum, who is a smoker, but nice. As far as I could see, she doesn't deserve a son like Tony, who was very rude to her. I caught Mum shaking her head over this more than once. Mum didn't get along too well with any of these people, incidentally: Tammy's mum was too shy, Angus's dad was too silent, Tony's mum allowed her son to get away with murder, and Amy's dad, according to my mum, was a 'sleazebag'. So Mum talked mostly to Mrs Patel, our teacher, when the poor thing could spare a moment. She was kept pretty busy during the bus trip, separating troublemakers, rounding up strays and cleaning up puke. Like I said before, it was a horrible trip.

So why were we all there? It wasn't as if we *had* to go. Well – I told you why Amy was there: so that she could flirt with Jesse. Jesse was there (I later found out), not because he was interested in history, but because his older brother Raphael had gone on a similar excursion once, and had managed to persuade some kindly farmer to buy him a bottle of booze at the Royal Hotel. No doubt Jesse was hoping that he himself would have the same kind of luck. And it must have been Jesse who persuaded Malcolm Morling and Tony Karavias to come along too. They're his gang; he never seems to go anywhere without them.

As for me, I'm the *last* person you would have expected to see on a camping trip. I certainly didn't want to go, not at first. But when my mum found Mrs Patel's crumpled note at the bottom of my school bag, she got all excited.

'This sounds good, Allie,' she said. (I should explain that my mum's a bit of a hippy; hence the fact that my name's Alethea, which means 'truth' in Greek, and my brother's name is Bethan, which means 'life' in Welsh.) 'Would you like to go to Hill End? We could manage it, I'm sure.'

'No, thank you,' I replied.

'Oh, come on. It's supposed to be a wonderful place. Very historic.'

'I know.' Mrs Patel had been talking about it for weeks. Everyone in my class had been told, over and

4

over again, that Hill End used to have twenty-eight hotels during the Gold Rush era, when thousands of people were digging in the mines surrounding the town. Now there's only one hotel and a thin scattering of houses. But because all those houses are very old and historic, and because you can still see traces of the nineteenth-century mines, a lot of tourists go to Hill End. A lot of tourists, a lot of artists, and a lot of school students whose teachers think that it might be a good educational experience to explore a genuine Gold Rush town.

'It would only be for two nights,' Mum mused, poring over the fine print on Mrs Patel's note. 'Ray's got all that camping gear he uses when he goes out to draw trees for the Department of Forestry. I'm sure he wouldn't mind lending it to us.'

'What do you mean, to *us*?' I demanded. 'You won't be going.'

'Oh, I think I might. I've always wanted to go to Hill End.'

'But it's a school excursion, Mum!'

'Yes, but Mrs Patel says here that she can't get any other teachers to help out, so she's asking for parents to volunteer as supervisors. I wouldn't mind doing that.'

'But, *Mum*,' I wailed, 'it's *camping*! You hate camping!'

'No, I don't. What gave you that idea?'

'*You* did! When we went camping last time! You said that you would never, ever do it again!'

'Oh, Allie.' Mum laughed. 'That was nearly five years ago. You were only seven, then, and Bethan was only three. Of course it was a bad experience. I should never have taken you both – you were much too young.'

'But –'

'I used to love camping, before you were born. Your father and I used to spend weeks in the Blue Mountains, communing with nature. Of course,' she added snippily, in the tone of voice that she always uses when she talks about my dad, 'I was the one who organised all the supplies and everything. Jim seemed to think that he could live out there under bits of bark, eating bush food. If it weren't for me, he would have died of exposure.'

I'm always confused when Mum starts to talk about Dad. He lives in Thailand now; I haven't seen him since I was four, though he phones us once a month. Mum doesn't mention him often, but when she does she gets this sarcastic note in her voice. Then I feel as if I want to defend him, but how can I? Because I don't really know him.

So I tend to shut up and say nothing. That's why Mum won the argument about the camping trip, and I had to face the horrible prospect of two nights spent in a sleeping bag.

But as the trip drew closer, I began to think that it might not be so bad after all. For one thing, Bethan wasn't invited. He's still only eight, and it was a Year

Six excursion, so he had to stay at home with Ray for the weekend. Poor Ray. Bethan has cricket on Saturday mornings, and likes to practise his bowling up at the local nets on Saturday afternoons. What's more, on Sundays he takes his skateboard down to the park whenever he can find someone older to go along with him. (Mum won't let him go, otherwise.) So poor Ray had a miserable weekend, on account of the fact that he's an artist, and hates all sport. Won't even watch the footy. I've known him for five years now, ever since Mum first met him, and in all that time he's never once shown the slightest interest in any kind of sporting event. When the Olympics were on he shut himself in his studio, with earplugs in his ears.

It's amazing that he and Bethan get on so well.

Another good thing about the trip was that Michelle decided to come. Michelle is my best friend. Though she reads books (like me), and gets high marks in geometry and maths, she's also a very stylish girl, and rarely leaves her house without putting on earrings and hand cream and toenail polish. That's why I hadn't expected her to sign up for the Hill End excursion. Somehow I couldn't picture her in a tent, or a public shower block.

'It's my mum,' she explained to me.

'Your mum?'

'She's got a new boyfriend, and she wants to go away with him for the weekend. That's why she wants *me* to go away.'

'Oh.'

'She's bought me a whole new tent,' Michelle said plaintively, 'and now she says that I have to learn to put it up. How will I ever learn to put it up? I can't even put up my Barbie swimming pool.'

'You won't need a tent,' I pointed out. 'You can sleep in ours. It's huge – it sleeps four people. It's got a door and a window and everything.'

Michelle looked at me doubtfully. I don't think she's ever slept in a room with anyone. (She's an only child.) But when I told her about Ray's portable gas stove, and fold-out camp chairs, and the insulated ground sheet, she agreed to share our tent. As a result, she didn't have to bring along anything except her clothes, her toiletries and her sleeping bag, which was a fancy one made for mountain climbers or Arctic explorers – I can't remember which. You were supposed to be able to roll it up so that it would fit in a tube about the size of a large container of Sara Lee chocolate ice-cream. Once we'd unrolled it, however, we were never able to fit it back into its little blue tube. We had a hard time fitting it back into the *bus*, let alone the tube.

But Michelle's sleeping bag isn't important. I'm only talking about it because I don't know how to tell you the real reason I went on that trip. It's very embarrassing, and I'm ashamed of myself for being such a hopeless idiot, but the fact is that at the time of our Hill End trip, like just about every other girl in Year

Six, I had a crush on Jesse Gerangelos. Yes, that's right. The same Jesse Gerangelos whose brother got expelled for setting fire to the school gym mats. The same Jesse Gerangelos who climbed on top of the assembly hall roof. The same Jesse Gerangelos who called me a loony-tune when it first got around that our house was haunted – that Jesse Gerangelos. You might be asking: what's wrong with you, Allie? What the hell did you see in that stirrer? Well, for one thing I saw someone who isn't by any means a fool, despite the fact that he hangs out with yobbos. You might disagree with this, but I assure you, he's not stupid; that poem he wrote about underpants, for Mrs Patel – it might have been rude, but it was actually quite clever. (And it was clever, too, the way he acted up until Mrs Patel asked him to read out his homework poem, or hadn't he done it? I'm sure she's regretted that request ever since.) Don't get me wrong; I could have written that poem myself, easily. But I'm not so good at making snappy jokes, and Jesse is. Once, when I passed Jesse and his mates sitting on the stairs near the assembly hall, Tony Karavias cried out: 'Hey, Allie Gebhardt! Have you ever worn a bikini?' Whereupon Jesse, quick as a flash, turned to him and said: 'Why? Have you?'

Of course, everyone laughed at Tony – which is perhaps the reason why Jesse made his comment in the first place. I don't suppose he was trying to do *me* a favour. But it was smart, I thought. And helpful. And

9

it made me wonder if perhaps Jesse wasn't a *total* dead-head. It even made me wonder if he liked me a little bit. Just a tiny, weeny bit. And when you start thinking like that, it isn't long before you find yourself watching that person out of the corner of your eye, and wondering where he is if you can't see him, and laughing at all his jokes (even if they're sometimes a bit dumb), and admiring the way he wears his school shirts all loose and floppy, and wishing that he would sit next to you instead of Amy Driscoll . . . that sort of thing.

Besides, you have to admit that Jesse's good-looking. *Very* good-looking. Even now, though I'm well and truly over him, I can't deny that he has the longest eyelashes, the biggest eyes, the cheekiest smile and the most gorgeous hair of any boy I've every met. That smile, especially – I still can't get over how cute that smile is. It's so big and mischievous and sweet and rueful and appealing and crazy, all at the same time. How can one pair of dimples and one crooked canine tooth combine to create something that completely overturns your common sense? I don't know. It's a mystery. But it's the sort of mystery that people are always complaining about in books and pop songs – the mystery of the human heart. So it's not *my* fault that I went a bit stupid. It could have happened to anyone. It happened to Michelle a little while back, and she's normally the most sensible person in the world when it comes to boys.

Anyway, that's the third reason why I was feeling positive about this trip — because Jesse was going. I figured that, even if it was a total disaster, only good would come of sitting around a campfire with Jesse Gerangelos, or sleeping near him under the stars. God, I was stupid. I can't bear to think about how stupid I was. I knew *perfectly well* that he couldn't be trusted, that he was always mucking about, that he probably wasn't interested in me — or in anything much, except his brothers' cars — and I was still pining after him.

You'd think that I would have known better, especially since Jesse and his mates were one of the main reasons why our bus trip was so awful. Another reason was that us kids didn't get along much better than the adults. We all ended up in the usual groups, and didn't mix despite the best efforts of Mrs Patel, who's always forcing kids like Tammy to work in project teams with kids like Amy. Poor Tammy — she didn't want anything to *do* with Amy, who of course stuck close to Jesse, Tony and Malcolm. Zoe did whatever Amy did. Angus and Serge were inseparable, as always. And Peter Cresciani followed me around — I don't know why. Perhaps it was because his mates hadn't come. Perhaps he found Angus and the other boys a bit dull, though Angus's dad was the one who obviously felt responsible for Peter, helping him to pitch his tent and fry his bread. Whatever the reason, Peter always seemed to be hovering nearby, a red baseball cap pulled down low over his nose and a backpack slung over one shoulder.

Not that I minded. Peter's a nice enough bloke. I just wasn't used to him, or his deadpan sense of humour. And I've always been a bit wary of fanatical science-fiction types.

'I think we've fallen into a time warp,' he remarked, when we were sitting around the Village Camping Area, eating a late lunch. 'Maybe we should recalibrate our temporal dislocation signatures.'

'*What?*' said Michelle.

'I just mean that it all looks very old,' Peter explained. 'Don't you think?'

I surveyed the Village Camping Area, which was a grassy spot down near the river, enclosed by a post-and-rail fence. Around us stood many shady trees, a handful of green garbage bins, some power sockets for caravans and a scattering of picnic benches. There was also a collection of brick barbecues, and a large building with a tin roof that contained septic toilets and coin-operated hot showers.

'Old?' I said. 'Do you think so?'

'Not *here*,' said Peter. 'Obviously I don't mean *here*. I mean the town. The buildings.'

I thought about the glimpses that we'd caught of Hill End, coasting down the main road towards the river. It certainly wasn't anything like Sydney. Ringed by scrubby hills, it was all rickety picket fences, overgrown vacant lots and dirt lanes. The houses had rusty tin roofs and crumbling chimneys, and often looked as if they'd been tacked together out of corrugated iron, mud bricks and firewood. On the outskirts of town the sun beat down out of an intensely blue sky onto patches of orange earth scored with deep crevices. Cows wandered about under poplar trees opposite a two-storey shop selling gold pans and camping gear. The Royal Hotel – scene of Jesse's brother's famous liquor purchase – loomed massively over everything, a line of cars nudging its front verandah like horses lined up eagerly at a trough.

'It's different,' I admitted.

'I wonder what will happen if it rains?' Michelle said uneasily, glancing at the cloudless sky. 'Do you think we'll be able to stay at the hotel?'

'It won't rain,' Mum assured her. I was beginning to wonder, with some alarm, if Mum was going to be dogging my steps for the entire weekend. (I mean, it was embarrassing enough that she'd come on the trip at all.) So far she hadn't seemed particularly interested in finding her own fun – but then again, we hadn't had a chance to do much, except pitch the tent and break out the sandwiches. Perhaps, I thought, things will change when we start trudging around with our project sheets. Surely Mum wouldn't want to hang out with us while we investigated wattle and daub construction and damp course lines?

But then again, since the Eglantine business she *had* been getting a bit more keen on history. That's one reason why she'd come to Hill End in the first place.

'So what are you going to do, Mum, while we're at the museum?' I asked. 'I think Tony's mum is going to do some sunbaking. Is that what you're going to do?'

'Sunbaking! I can do that any time.'

'There's some sort of antique shop up there,' I added cunningly. 'And an arts and crafts shop next to the general store.'

'No, no. I think I'll check out the museum. I'm supposed to be supervising, remember.'

'But –'

'I can't miss the Visitor Centre, anyway,' she concluded. 'I want to pick up maps and stuff. Besides, who knows? I might learn something.'

She was right, as it happened. She did learn something – in fact we both did.

We learned that there was a resident ghost at the Hill End museum.

CHAPTER # two

I forgot to mention that our bus driver, Steve, had been hired for the whole weekend. He'd been paid extra so that he could stay at the Royal Hotel; unlike the rest of us, he wasn't forced to pitch a tent or unroll a sleeping bag. We never saw him in the evenings, because he would retire to the pub at five o'clock. But during the day he was always available to drive us around in his bus – which he generally parked near the Village Camping Area.

On Friday afternoon, he drove us up to the Hill End Museum and Visitor Centre. It didn't take long. With a great hissing of brakes and grinding of gears he hauled us to the top of a hill overlooking the town, where we found a large, single-storey brick building with a wrap-around verandah.

'Okay now, everyone – quiet please!' Mrs Patel declared, as we gathered at the foot of the building's front steps. 'This is the old district hospital, and it dates from 1873. Malcolm, if you don't calm down, I'm going to put you back on the bus. If you look at your project sheet, you'll see questions about some of the exhibits in here – that's *enough*, Tony – so I want you to pay special attention to what you see. I want all those questions answered.'

'Mrs Patel!'

'What is it, Amy?'

'I need to go to the toilet.'

'There's a toilet inside.'

Normally Mrs Patel is a very calm sort of person, but I could see that even she was beginning to crumble under the strain. Her nail polish was beginning to chip. Her voice was beginning to crack. The long, black braid that hung down her back was beginning to unravel.

'There are several rooms inside, and I want you to have a careful look at the Village Room, which is room number one, as well as the Hospital Room –'

'Mrs Patel.'

'*What*? What is it *now*?'

'Zoe wants to go to the toilet too.'

'Zoe can go when you're finished, Amy. *Only* when you're finished.'

It's always the same. Whenever there's something

interesting to look at on a school excursion, the deadheads usually manage to spoil it by giggling and pushing and asking stupid questions about toilets. To tell you the truth, I don't really notice it any more, though I could see Mum rolling her eyes. Amy's dad whispered something to Tammy's mother, who gave a half-hearted smile. Then we all trooped into the museum.

It was dim and cavernous, with shiny bare floors and thick, heavy doorframes. The rooms opened off a central hall. No sooner had we clattered over the threshold than a blonde woman in a National Parks and Wildlife uniform emerged from the first room on our right, which contained racks of brochures, leaflets and souvenirs. Having introduced herself as Karen Smythe, she consulted Mrs Patel in a low voice about entry fees.

The rest of us waited. Our rubber soles squeaked on the polished floor and our voices echoed off the high ceiling. Jesse headed straight for the Visitors' Book. Surreptitiously, he picked up a pen and scribbled something in it. Then he showed his written comment to Malcom, who sniggered.

It always pained me to see Jesse acting like that. I was sure that, deep inside, he was capable of more mature behaviour.

'You people can just go ahead,' Mrs Patel suddenly remarked, breaking off her conversation with Karen Smythe. 'I'll be with you in a minute.'

'And if there's anything you want to know,' Karen added, 'feel free to ask. I'm here to answer any questions you might have.'

'Where are the toilets?' Tony Karavias piped up, from the back of the group. There was a ripple of laughter. But Karen Smythe remained serene.

'They're over there,' she said, pointing.

'*One at a time*,' Mrs Patel barked, as a good third of our group surged in the direction indicated. 'Amy, you first. The rest of you, start in room one. That's the Village Room.'

'Oh, boy,' Michelle murmured. 'Do we have to? Can't we start at the other end? I want to avoid all the drongos.'

She glanced at Mrs Patel, who was already moving away. Our teacher apparently had business to transact with Karen Smythe, in the room where Karen's cash register was nestled among the leaflets and brochures.

'I'm sure it won't matter,' Mum suddenly remarked. She was standing right behind me, and sounded fragile. 'I'm sure it won't matter if you start in this room over here. Not if I'm with you.'

She was obviously just as anxious to dodge the rest of the party as Michelle was. I understood how they both felt, though at the same time I was strangely reluctant to let Jesse out of my sight. It was stupid, of course; there wasn't any chance that he'd actually talk to me, or anything. So I fought against my secret crush, and followed Mum and Michelle into a room that was full of dusty old photographs. Most of them were photographs of past inhabitants of Hill End. Michelle and I carefully scanned our project sheets while Mum peered at the walls.

'I don't know,' said Michelle doubtfully, her voice hushed. 'I don't see any questions about anything in this room, do you?'

'I don't think so.'

'*Who laid the hospital's foundation stone and what else is he famous for?*' she read aloud. 'Maybe that's here somewhere. Can you see?'

'Oh, look!' Mum exclaimed. 'Look, Allie, this guy isn't white *or* Chinese. James Evans, goldminer, born 1829–31, arrived in Australia 1852. Isn't that interesting? I didn't know there *were* any black people on the goldfields. Apart from the Aborigines, of course.'

'Mmmm.'

'And look at this. Somebody called Red Jack Ellis with Bill Peach. Bill Peach must have made a show about him. I wonder why?'

'Who's Bill Peach?' I wanted to know, and Mum explained that he'd been a television presenter back in the 70s, when she was young. She couldn't remember the name of his program, but he'd gone all around Australia looking for interesting people.

'Like Red Jack Ellis, whoever he was,' she said, and jumped as Karen Smythe spoke behind her. None of us had heard anyone come in.

'Red Jack was a local character,' Karen announced. 'He was prospecting here till he died a few years ago. Prospecting for gold.'

'You mean people still do that?' I queried, and she laughed.

'Do they ever!'

'You mean – like mining?'

'No, not so much like mining,' Karen admitted. 'More like fossicking. Panning for gold. You can go on special fossicking tours, down around Tambaroora.'

'I think that's what we're doing tomorrow,' Michelle observed. 'I think I heard Mrs Patel say something about it.'

'There's an old bloke you see in the Golden Gully area who spends all his time fossicking,' Karen went on. 'Been there donkey's years – lives out in the bush some-where. *He's* one of the genuine old-timers, like Red Jack. You get the odd feral, around here.'

'And what about this guy?' Mum interrupted. 'James Evans? What's his significance?'

'Oh, now he was an interesting bloke,' Karen replied, her broad, freckled face becoming more animated. 'He came out here from America and married one of the hospital matrons – Elizabeth Evans. Granny Evans. Our resident ghost.'

I must have jumped halfway to the ceiling. Even Mum jerked her head. We're not like other people any more, you see; we can't hear the word 'ghost' without getting a little shock.

'What ghost?' I said sharply.

'There's a ghost here?' Mum gasped.

Though Michelle cast me a nervous glance, Karen didn't seem to notice our reaction. She spoke casually, her eyes fixed on the photo of James Evans, a smile lingering in the corners of her mouth. It was a slightly embarrassed smile.

'There's supposed to be a ghost,' she said. 'Old Granny Evans – she's still pacing the wards, apparently.'

'Why?' I demanded. 'Did she die here?'

'I don't think so . . .'

'Was she here a very long time?'

'I don't know. Maybe. There's a picture of her in the Hospital Room. She had nine children.' The smile had gone; perhaps our serious expressions had driven it away. 'People are supposed to have heard ghostly footsteps, though *I* never have.'

'Has anyone heard anything else?' I inquired. 'Or seen anything?'

'No . . .'

'No writing on the walls?' Michelle blurted out, and I shot her a warning look. I didn't want anyone to mention Eglantine. The minute you do that, people start to think you're a real wacko.

'N-n-o-o . . .' Karen raised an eyebrow. 'What do you mean? What kind of writing?'

'Oh – nothing,' I said quickly. 'Come on, Michelle. I don't think there's anything else in here that we need.'

I hustled her out the door and down the hallway. From the noise they were making, I deduced that our classmates were still in the Village Room, so I steered clear of them.

'What's the matter?' Michelle hissed. 'Why are you acting so funny?'

'I don't like people talking about Eglantine.'

'Why not?'

'You *know*.' I had told her about all the kids teasing me – about Jesse Gerangelos calling me a loony-tune. I couldn't believe that she was even asking. 'When you talk about ghosts, Michelle, everyone thinks you're a nutcase.'

'But that woman was talking about the Granny ghost –'

'Yes, but it's not the *same*. Eglantine was real. No one seems to know if this one is real or not.' I stopped abruptly. 'Look,' I said. 'The Hospital Room. Let's check it out.'

'Okay. If you want.'

It was a small room, painted white. There was an old-fashioned hospital bed in the middle of it, and bits of antique medical equipment arranged on shelves and in cupboards: frightening surgical instruments, ominous rubber hoses, poisonous-looking patent medicines. A nineteenth-century chart of the human body hung beside yet more dusty photographs. An oddly shaped enamel basin made me slightly uneasy – I don't know why.

'Yuk,' said Michelle, with a grimace. 'I bet some-body died in here. I bet *lots* of people died in here.'

'Patients, yes,' I agreed. 'So why is the ghost a nurse?'

'Maybe she was an evil nurse. Maybe she killed someone.'

'Maybe.'

'Look! Is that her?'

It was. Elizabeth Evans, died September 1929 – the same year the hospital closed. Matron of the hospital from 1889 until 1895. She had a face like a hatchet.

At that point, a swelling tide of noise warned us that the Hospital Room was about to be invaded. Sure enough, we suddenly found ourselves sur-rounded by the people we'd been trying to escape.

'Oh! Gross!' yelped Zoe Mylchreest, having spotted the surgical instruments.

'*When did the hospital close?*' Angus mumbled, reading aloud from his project sheet.

'Hello,' said Peter Cresciani, nudging me in the ribs. 'Where did you guys get to?'

Jesse and his gang, I noticed, were thoroughly preoccupied with a plaster model of the inner ear; I wondered what Jesse was saying that seemed to be so funny. Michelle, however, wasn't interested. She dragged me into the Village Room, which was now empty except for one poor tourist whose visit had – unfortunately for him – coincided with our school's.

(I noticed that he didn't hang around for too long.) Michelle and I were therefore able to study the exhibits in peace, answering all Mrs Patel's questions about mining equipment, local newspapers, domestic life and transport. We then moved on to look at the replica of a mining registrar's office, the panoramic views of nineteenth century Hill End, the gallery of past notables, and the set of antique beer taps. It was all very interesting, but my thoughts kept straying to the mystery of Elizabeth Evans. Was she really haunting the old hospital? If so, how had she been recognised as Elizabeth Evans? It isn't easy, identifying ghosts. It takes a lot of research.

Perhaps, I thought, if there *is* a ghost, it's not the ghost of Elizabeth Evans at all. Perhaps it's actually one of the patients who died here, and people assume that it's Granny Evans because of the way it paces around. Matrons always pace around.

'Did that National Parks woman say anything else about the ghost?' I asked my mother in a low voice, as we waited to board the bus.

'No,' she replied softly. She looked a bit subdued.

'I wonder if there really is one.'

Mum tucked a strand of fluffy red hair behind one ear. Whenever she fiddles with her hair, I know that she's nervous.

'The *bagua* alignment in that place is shocking,' she said obscurely, and I sighed. Feng Shui again. Mum is

24

devoted to Feng Shui. It's a Chinese philosophy that tells you how to rearrange your house for good luck.

'You mean the Feng Shui's so bad that there's bound to be ghosts?' I asked.

'I don't know. I don't know enough about it.'

'I wonder if Richard Boyer would be interested?' Richard is our friend from PRISM – which stands for Paranormal Research Investigation Services and Monitoring. When Eglantine was haunting our house, he was one of the people who tried to work out why; he's fascinated by the paranormal, you see, though he actually works for some sort of computer company. (He only does things for PRISM in his spare time.) It was Richard who got film of Eglantine's spirit-writing as it slowly appeared on my brother's bedroom wall – though he never did offer us any kind of theory about why Eglantine couldn't seem to rest in peace. I was the one who solved that puzzle. And Delora Starburn, the psychic, was the one who gave Eglantine what she wanted, so that she stopped haunting our house.

As a matter of fact, Richard met Delora at our place, and they started going out together soon after that. Nowadays Delora is an enthusiastic member of PRISM. Mum says that Eglantine played cupid with Richard and Delora; she also says that their love affair 'can't possibly last'. But when I ask her why, she just mutters something about how I wouldn't understand.

As a matter of fact, I probably would understand. Jesse and I are a bad match, too.

'Mum?' I said. 'What do you think? Should we tell Richard?'

'Oh, I don't know. Maybe.'

'I bet Delora would have a great time in there. I bet she'd pick up all kinds of vibes.'

'I don't need Delora to tell me this place is full of negative energy,' Mum retorted. 'Stop talking about ghosts, Allie, would you? It's too late in the day.'

'But –'

'I've told you before, it's not healthy. Spiritually, it's not healthy. Now are you going to get off at the general store with me, or continue on to the camping ground? I need to buy some milk and sausages for everyone.'

'Camping ground, please.' I didn't want to be hanging out with Mum all the time. Besides, I knew that Jesse would be there, and I wanted to keep an eye on him. Not talk to him, or anything. Not follow him around. Just keep an eye on him.

So when Mum hopped off the bus at the Royal Hotel, I stayed in my seat. Michelle and I rode the bus all the way to the camping ground, where we sat outside our tent and talked about Elizabeth Evans as the shadows grew long, and the air cooler. I was poking at the earth with a stick, and glancing over to where Jesse, Malcolm and Tony were fooling around near the most far-flung barbecue. The two dads were trying to light this barbecue with matches and heat beads and bits of dry bark; I had a horrible feeling that, with the Three Stooges getting in their way, there was bound to be a nasty accident.

'The thing with Eglantine,' I said slowly, 'is that she not only died in our house – she died before she could finish something. Her book. It was really, really important to her. So what's important enough to keep Granny Evans pacing around the hospital?'

Michelle pondered. 'Maybe she was fired,' she said at last. 'Maybe she didn't want to leave, so now she's back.'

'Who's back?' a voice interrupted. We looked around, and saw Peter Cresciani approaching us. He came and sat down beside me, slinging his backpack onto the ground. 'Are you talking about your mum?'

'No.' I peered at the main gate, then at the darkening sky. 'But speaking of my mum, I wonder where she is? It shouldn't take this long to buy a carton of milk.'

'It's probably that time vortex again,' Peter observed calmly, rummaging in his bag for a muesli bar. 'She's probably fallen through it, and now she's stuck in the 1870s.'

'Don't be stupid,' I said. 'My mum's already in a time vortex. She still listens to all this terrible 70s music.'

'Well, she'd better be back before it gets dark,' Peter went on, through a mouthful of muesli bar. 'Because it's my theory that every night this entire town goes back in time, to the Gold Rush era, and you're only safe if you're sitting here, in the triangle made by those three green garbage bins. The ones that look like R2-D2. They're obviously pieces of technology left here aeons ago by visiting aliens.'

I couldn't help smiling. 'Peter,' I began, 'you are such a lunatic.' But before I could say any more, Michelle suddenly raised her hand and pointed.

'Look!' she exclaimed. 'Isn't that your mum getting out of a car?'

It was. She was getting out of a beat-up old red car. For a moment we could only see her backside, because she had her head in the car and was talking to the driver. Then she straightened up, slammed the front passenger door, and stood with her back to us, waving, as the car drove off.

'Weird,' I muttered.

'Who was that behind the wheel?' Michelle asked.

'I don't know.'

'Maybe your mum hitched a lift,' Peter suggested.

'From the store?' It didn't seem likely. The store was only about ten minutes walk away. 'Why would she do that? She's always telling me never to hitchhike.' I watched her come trotting towards us, her hair bouncing and her earrings jangling. She had a big smile on her face.

'Allie!' she cried when we were in earshot. 'You'll never guess! That was Samantha Cornish!'

I stared at her blankly.

'You remember Samantha!' Her voice was breathless and impatient. 'She married Hessel Venclovas! He's an artist and she's a potter.'

'You mean they're friends of Ray's?' I hazarded.

'Oh, come on, Allie, you must remember *something* about them. We visited them once on the Hawkesbury. They had that house beside the water.'

'Oh.' A memory stirred. 'The one with the oyster-shell wall?'

'That's it!' Mum swung around to address Michelle. 'We lost track of them a couple of years ago, when their phone was disconnected,' she explained. 'But it turns out they live here, now, in Hill End.' Turning back to me, she added: 'And they've invited us to dinner! Isn't that *great?*'

Trust Mum. Wherever we go, no matter how remote, there's always some old hippy friend of hers who wants to feed us millet and lentil casserole.

I've got used to it by now.

CHAPTER # three

As a matter of fact, I was wrong. Samantha and Hessel didn't serve us millet and lentil casserole for dinner. Instead, we had chicken cacciatore and rice, with a rocket salad and homemade apple pie. But they were still hippies, even so. Only hippies would spend more than one minute in Taylor's Cottage.

There was no electricity. The water came out of a tank. The bathroom was a shed made of corrugated iron – even the chimney was made of corrugated iron – and you had to cook on a wood stove. The ceilings were covered with white cloth instead of plaster, and the dunny was out in the backyard. Yet Samantha and Hessel were proud of this awful place. When Mum and I arrived with Michelle, our hosts dragged us all over the house, pointing out the 'classic split-slab construction', the original floorboards, the claw-footed bath, the fireplaces, the oil lamps, the meat safe that had 'come with the house', the flour bags tacked over one wall.

'It's genuine – absolutely genuine,' Samantha gushed.

'As stewards, we pay a nominal rent to National Parks and Wildlife, and ensure that the integrity of the structure is maintained,' said Hessel. 'No intrusive additions. No aluminium windows or television aerials. We preserve it as it should be preserved.'

'But – but doesn't it get *cold*?' I stammered, eyeing the gaps between the tin roof of the kitchen and the top of its walls.

'Oh no!' Samantha laughed. 'Not with our wonderful old fireplaces!' And she started to talk about the quality of the dead wood that she found while roaming through the bush around Hill End. 'Dry as tinder,' she said, 'but so beautifully shaped that I sometimes can't bring myself to burn it!'

Mum, of course, lapped all this up – even though she couldn't have endured one night in Taylor's Cottage. Her blood circulation is too bad. But she understood where Samantha was coming from; they're two of a kind in some ways. Samantha is small and dark, with brown skin and a dried-up face, while Mum is tall and pale and freckled. But they both like wearing bright silk scarves, and chunky jewellery, and ethnic sandals, and the sort of clothes you buy at markets (homemade stuff covered in splatter-painting or ink-block shapes or Indian embroidery). What's more, Mum admires Samantha's pots, which are always a very intense blue or an equally vivid orange, so pure and clean that they almost seem to glow. Hessel, on the other hand, paints splodgy abstract paintings, and Mum doesn't like them. She says that abstract shapes create an environment in which people find it hard to finish things. That's why she likes Ray's work, because Ray paints things that you can recognise.

I don't think Mum admires anything much about Hessel, to tell you the truth. He's kind of fat and slobby, with a beard that looks as if it could do with a good mow. He doesn't talk much, but when he does he seems to think that he's doing everyone a big favour. And I noticed that he didn't lift *one finger* to help Samantha with dinner, except to light the candles. Mum noticed that, too; I could tell. She and Ray always share the cooking.

'So what brought you here, Sam?' she asked brightly, when Samantha finally sat down to eat. 'What brought you to Hill End?'

'Oh, Judy, it was like coming home,' Samantha replied. 'The affinity we have with this place – it's like we've been here before, isn't it, Hessel?'

A grunt from Hessel.

'I've never seen any other white man's settlement in this country that's so at peace with the land it's occupying,' Samantha went on. 'The feeling of continuity, of *heart's ease*, that's grown out of exile – it invests everything that I do here.'

'And the light,' said Hessel, through a mouthful of chicken.

'And the light,' Samantha agreed. 'And the textures. We had to stay. We didn't have a choice. Did we, Hessel?'

They raved about their wonderful life in Hill End for hours, while night fell, and Michelle stifled her yawns, and my feet got colder and colder. I'd never wanted to join the grown-ups for dinner in the first place. I'd wanted to eat barbecued sausages with Jesse at the camping ground, and was wondering if I should give Mum a kick or a nudge (it was half past nine, after all), when suddenly Samantha said something that made my heart skip a beat.

'. . . and of course there's our ghost,' she trilled, sounding just the tiniest bit anxious but trying to cover it up. 'We have a ghost, you know. According to our next-door neighbour.'

Mum and Michelle and I just sat with our mouths open. *Another* ghost? We couldn't believe our ears.

'Oh, yes,' Samantha continued, with a little laugh. 'Many's the time we've come home to find a bottle smashed, or a small pile of objects stacked on the bottom shelf of the bookcase. Our neighbour Alf says that it's the ghost of a former occupant. Little Eustace Harrow, he says.'

'Eustace Harrow?' I couldn't resist pressing her. 'Who was he?'

'Well, according to Alf, he was the son of the woman who used to live here. The woman who died. Evie Harrow. She lived here for eighty-three years, would you believe it? Born and died in this very house.'

I shuddered. Eighty-three years in *this* place! Michelle and I exchanged horrified looks.

'Evie was married and had two kids,' Samantha informed us, 'but the youngest died when he was only three years old. Eustace, his name was. Alf maintains that his ghost has been haunting the place ever since he died here.'

'Oh,' said Mum. She cast a troubled glance around the gloomy, draughty kitchen, with its rusty old biscuit tins and dangling copper pots and brooding meat safe. 'He died right here, did he?'

'That's what Alf says,' Samantha confirmed. 'Anyone for coffee?'

'Coffee,' Hessel barked.

'Oh – thanks, Sam. Coffee would be nice,' said Mum.

'And what about you girls? Coffee? Tea? I have herbal tea.'

'No, thanks.'

'No, thanks.'

'Are you sure? What about cocoa? I think I have some cocoa somewhere . . .'

'No, thanks,' I repeated. 'Um – what else did Alf tell you? About this ghost?'

Samantha looked slightly surprised that I should be pursuing the subject. But she got up and began to potter about, running water into a kettle (the pipes made a noise like someone driving a truck full of kitchenware repeatedly into a metal street-lamp) and noisily rearranging logs in the stove.

'Well, he hasn't told us much,' she said, raising her voice. 'He's a real country character – a man of few words. Isn't that right, Hessel?'

Another grunt from Hessel.

'But we were asking him about this odd little pile of coins and keys and pebbles we'd found in one of the old kitchen cabinets – oh, yes, we had those cabinets torn out, they were from the 1960s, they weren't in character – and he told us that Eustace was always one for collecting funny little oddments, and stacking them in out-of-the-way places,' Samantha went on. 'Used to do it when he was alive, apparently. That's why Evie knew that he was still around, after he died – because she kept on finding these piles of buttons and hairpins and peanut shells. That kind of thing.'

'Oh, dear,' said Mum. 'How sad. How awful.' Her eyes filled with tears, and Samantha looked at her in surprise.

'Well – I suppose so,' she conceded. 'Though Evie seemed to find it a comfort. At least Alf says she did.'

'And that's what you've been finding?' I queried. 'Little piles of . . . things?'

'With no logic to them,' Samantha agreed. 'We use powdered milk here, Judy, since there's no refrigerator. Is that all right with you?'

'Yes, thanks.'

'It's amazing what you can do without, if you put your mind to it,' Samantha burbled on. 'I've found a marvellous way of keeping cheese fresh for days and days – I got it out of an old book of household management –'

'But what kinds of things have you found?' I interrupted, impatient to hear the rest of the story. 'Bones? Rocks? Feathers?'

'Oh, just things from around the house. A paperclip, maybe, and a pair of tweezers. A book of stamps. A salt cellar. A piece of string. All jumbled together.'

'That's what Allie used to do, when she was little,' Mum suddenly remarked, her voice full of awe. 'Leave little caches of toys around the house. I'd always be finding plastic animals in the bread bin. Or doll's house furniture under the sink.'

'And there was a trail of throat lozenges left on the kitchen floor, once,' Samantha added. 'Plus we've had some mysterious breakages.'

'We had those, too, but they weren't so mysterious,' Mum said. 'They were Bethan's fault.'

'It *is* a bit annoying,' Samantha confessed, again with a laugh. She put a tray on the table, and passed around the hot drinks. Then she settled herself down with a mug of tea clasped between her hands, which had dry clay trapped in all their cracks and creases. 'I'm always losing things, though they turn up eventually, hidden away in the dresser or behind the couch. And the breakages *are* a pest. Two lamps, three beautiful antique dishes and a piece of Stuart crystal. Tragic losses, really.'

Mum cleared her throat.

'Do you – um – want to get rid of it?' she inquired, ignoring my scowl.

'The ghost, you mean?' Samantha couldn't seem to touch on the subject without breaking into that careless little laugh. 'Well, I don't see how. I use *heaps* of garlic in my cooking, don't I, Hessel? And if garlic drives vampires away, it should drive away ghosts, don't you think?' Laugh, laugh. 'And I can't exactly set a trap. Besides, Eustace is part of the house. We're supposed to be preserving the house. And he might be quite a drawcard, if we decide to open a Bed and Breakfast.'

'A Bed and Breakfast?' Mum echoed. Michelle blinked, and I nearly fell out of my chair. A Bed and Breakfast? In *this* house? I couldn't imagine that *anyone* would want to stay with Samantha and Hessel.

But Samantha began to talk about eco-tourism, and how people were becoming more and more open to the idea of hiring cabins in the bush, where they could commune with nature and get away from the pressures of modern life. Why not, in that case, cater for people who were looking for a truly authentic, historical experience? Without electricity? Without a telephone? Without anything that would spoil the nineteenth-century atmosphere of Taylor's Cottage?

'You don't have a phone?' asked Mum.

'No. It's quite wonderful,' Samantha replied. 'We get so much work done, don't we, Hessel?'

'Because I was thinking that, if you wanted me to, I could ring some friends of ours,' said Mum, for all the world as if I wasn't kicking her under the table. 'Richard Boyer and Delora Starburn. They helped us to get rid of the ghost in our house.'

'What?' Samantha gasped. Even Hessel shifted in his seat. 'What do you mean, Jude? You're not serious.'

'Yes! Absolutely! I know it sounds ridiculous, but there was no other explanation. Our house was haunted, wasn't it, Allie?'

I rolled my eyes. But it was no good – I couldn't stop her. Within minutes she had described the whole Eglantine business, to the obvious delight of Samantha, who kept yelping and gasping. 'But this is incredible!' she would shriek. 'Judy, you poor thing!' They finally fell to discussing purification rituals and negative energy flows, until Hessel said sharply that he wanted another cup of coffee.

'Maybe we could call these friends of yours,' Samantha exclaimed in eager tones, as she leapt up to fetch Hessel his coffee. 'Do you think they'd like to stay in the spare room? It's the one we've been hoping to use if we open a B & B – it's got that lovely old iron bedstead in it.'

'We could always ask them,' said Mum, no less eagerly. 'I'm sure they'd love to help. They're always looking for manifestations.'

'We could call them tomorrow, maybe. From the phone at the store.'

'Or I could call them now,' Mum suggested, groping around for her bag. 'I've got a mobile, you know.'

'A mobile!' Samantha threw up her hands. 'Judy, how can you? The radiation!'

'I know, I know.' Mum sounded ashamed. 'But with the kids and everything . . .'

'The kids are the ones you should be looking out for!'

'Excuse me, but no one's proved that mobile phones are bad for you,' I pointed out flatly. Then I turned to Mum. 'You can't call Richard, now,' I said, 'it's nearly ten.'

'Oh, he'll be up. He's a night owl.'

'But, Mum –'

'Shh!' She put a finger to her lips, and the phone to her ear. 'It's ringing!'

What is it about adults when they drink alcohol? Mum never lets *me* call people at ten p.m. But there Mum was, giggling into her mobile as she spoke to poor Richard, who was probably standing by the phone in his pyjamas, with his mouth full of toothpaste.

'It's *made* for you, this place, it's *crawling* with ghosts,' Mum enthused. 'Yes . . . yes . . . oh, well you might have heard of the one in the hospital. Granny Evans? The old matron? No? Well, there's that one and there's this one. A little boy, apparently. Son of the former owner. Yes. No, he leaves things in piles. Smashes things. What? I don't know. I don't know if you'd call him a poltergeist. They haven't actually seen him, but he's made his presence felt. Oh, it's the most *wonderful* house.' (I didn't dare look at Michelle when Mum said this.) 'An absolutely authentic miner's cottage. Oil lamps and everything. Yes. Yes. Oh, the weather's perfect. Couldn't be better.' A long pause. Bright-eyed, Mum nodded furiously at Samantha, and made thumbs-up signals. 'You will? Really? Both of you? Oh, that's fantastic. You'll love it. No, don't worry. Just stop at the store opposite the Royal Hotel, and ask the way to Taylor's Cottage. Everyone knows everyone around here. The Royal Hotel? Oh, you can't miss it. Honestly. It's the only one in town.'

So that's how Mum persuaded Richard and Delora to come down to Hill End for a night. Just one quick phone call and the deed was done. Later, as we walked back to the camping ground, I pointed out the obvious.

'Mum,' I said, 'how could you? Richard's our friend. He's a nice person. He's going to hate us, once he sees what you've got him into.'

'Don't be silly, Allie. He'll love Taylor's Cottage.'

'Mum! There's no electricity! The dunny's in the *garden.*'

'It's not very comfortable, Mrs Gebhardt,' Michelle agreed, backing me up. 'I wouldn't like to stay there myself.'

'That's because you girls are pampered television addicts and suburbanites, with no sense of adventure. Besides, Richard's always happy wherever there's a ghost. He'll sleep on a stone floor if it gives him the chance to monitor paranormal activity. He's not going to mind that Samantha doesn't have a fridge.'

I looked at Michelle and shrugged. There's no arguing with Mum, sometimes.

'I've never met Richard,' Michelle remarked. 'I've heard you talk about him lots of times, but I've never met him.'

'Haven't you?' I said.

'I think he was mostly around when you were trying to get rid of Eglantine,' Michelle continued, 'and you weren't talking about that much, I remember. You were too embarrassed.'

For a few minutes we walked on in silence, our feet crunching on gravel, our torches illuminating distant treetops and ramshackle picket fences. Bushes rustled to our right. A deep, thrumming call sounded to our left.

'Frogmouth?' Mum wondered aloud.

'Maybe it's a wallaby, or something.' I cleared my throat. 'So what do you think of this ghost, Mum? Do you think he's really real?'

'Oh, for God's *sake*, Allie, not *now*,' Mum protested, and I took her point. It *was* a bit spooky, walking along a chilly country road at night, with no houses in our immediate vicinity and no distant traffic noises to provide a comforting backdrop to the whisper of the breeze and the croaking of unseen creatures. Above us, dark, winged shapes passed overhead, dimly visible against the stars. A sheep cried out in the distance. By the time we reached our tent, we were almost – but not quite – running.

We didn't talk about Eustace again before going to bed. But I did think about him. I wondered why, if he actually existed, he was still hanging around Taylor's Cottage now that his mother was gone.

I also wondered how he had died. Burned in a fire? Drowned in a well? If he had died of an illness, he might have breathed his last in the spare room – the room that Richard was supposed to be sleeping in. Poor Richard. I felt so, so sorry for him.

But to be honest with you, I didn't spend much time sympathising with Richard, *or* thinking about Eustace. My head was filled with Jesse Gerangelos (as usual). I couldn't believe that he was sleeping in a tent not twenty metres away. I was disappointed that I had missed seeing him at dinner. And I kept dreaming about what might happen the next day, when I would be wandering around Hill End in his company.

Pathetic, isn't it?

CHAPTER # four

In case you ever decide to go camping, let me give you this advice: don't. Sleeping in a tent is no fun – especially when you're sleeping with my mother. (She makes funny snuffling noises.) Your face also gets very cold where it sticks out of the sleeping bag, and the birds always wake you up at the crack of dawn. I was awake at *half past five*, on Saturday morning. I couldn't believe it when I looked at my watch. And by the time I'd walked to the toilets and back, through the icy, dewy grass, I hadn't a chance of getting to sleep again. I was well and truly conscious.

So I dug out a box of Special K, and sat eating it dry while the sun rose. I was hoping that Jesse might be the next one to roll out of bed – that we might find ourselves eating breakfast together, without anyone else around. But of course I wasn't that lucky. The second person to wake up was Angus's dad, who immediately retreated into the shower block. Then Tammy appeared, and scurried off to visit the toilets. Then Peter crawled out of his tiny tent, and staggered over to where I was sitting. His brown hair was standing up all over his head.

'It's freezing,' he mumbled, wiping his nose on his wrist.

'Yes,' I replied.

'What are you eating?'

'Breakfast.'

'How was your dinner last night?'

'Okay.'

There was a brief silence. (I didn't want to talk about Eustace, because I'd copped enough heat at school over Eglantine.) After a few minutes Peter seemed to snap out of his trance; he turned on his heel and vanished. When I next saw him, he was washed and brushed and feeling better. That was at about nine o'clock; we were all milling around waiting for the bus to arrive, having eaten our breakfasts, brushed our teeth and packed our bags. Some of us – myself included – had even washed a few dishes.

Most of the adults, I might add, were looking like death, because no one had been able to light a fire to boil water to make coffee. Even Mrs Patel seemed a bit dazed.

'This is Jesse's chance,' Peter observed. He had attached himself to me, as usual, and was gazing over to where Jesse and Malcolm were fooling around with a long piece of rubber tyre, which they were cracking like a whip. 'He should make a break for it now, while the grown-ups are still suffering from coffee withdrawal symptoms. They'll never be able to catch him.'

'Don't be stupid,' I said.

'Did anyone see where Jesse got to last night?' Peter went on. 'Did he make it to the pub, do you think? He got up pretty late this morning. Did anyone smell alcohol on his breath?'

'No one with a hangover would be whipping a piece of tyre around like that,' I retorted. 'They'd be groaning and moaning and complaining about their headache. That's what Mum always does when she has a hangover.'

'True. That's true.' Peter folded his arms. 'I wonder where he got the tyre from? I wonder whose tyres he's been slashing? Maybe that's what he was doing last night – vandalising cars.'

'Oh, stop it,' I said crossly. I didn't like to hear anyone abusing Jesse. Nor did I wish to be persuaded that Jesse might have been making mischief. 'Look – here's the bus. It's about time.'

'So old Jess couldn't have been out slashing the *bus's* tyres, last night,' Peter murmured, but I ignored him. I climbed onto the bus and sat next to Michelle, who wasn't her usual well-groomed, glossy-haired self. She and I moaned about camping all the way to the graveyard at Tambaroora. She said that she had spent a dreadful night.

'All those insects flying around,' she complained. 'And my hair got caught in the zipper.'

'And it was so cold,' I added.

'Cold! Yes! And the *birds* . . .'

'Oh, my God. Don't talk to me about the birds. Weren't they *loud*?'

'You two sound like a pair of little old ladies,' my mum interrupted, from the seat behind us. 'It was a glorious night. It was beautiful.' This, mind you, from a woman whose eyes were all puffy and whose hands were trembling.

'It was awful,' I said stubbornly. 'I know you've got a headache, Mum – don't try and pretend you haven't.'

'That wasn't because I slept in a tent,' Mum rejoined. 'That was because I drank too much red wine last night. I always react badly to red wine.'

'Oh, yes!' said Mrs Patel, who was sitting beside her. 'How *was* your dinner party? Enjoyable?'

'Oh, it was marvellous! You should have seen the cottage, it was living history, no phone, no electricity, oil lamps, the most wonderful furniture, flour bags tacked over the walls, the most *spectacular* cottage garden . . .'

Michelle and I rolled our eyes. But Mum didn't have a chance to rave for long, because pretty soon we turned off Tambaroora Road and bumped up to the gate of the cemetery. The bus slowed. The engine died. Every nose was pressed against the window glass. 'Cool!' said Tony, from the back seat.

'We're not going to be here long,' Mrs Patel warned. 'No more than half an hour. So I want you to get stuck into those questions as quick as you can, please.'

'Mrs Patel?'

'What is it, Zoe?'

'I have to go to the toilet.'

Groan.

'Well, you're not doing it on consecrated ground,' Mrs Patel snapped. 'Everybody out, please. Hurry up. We haven't got all day.'

The Hill End and Tambaroora cemetery was a small, flat clearing hacked out of the bush. There was a bit of brick wall by the entrance, where the iron gates were painted white; elsewhere the fence around the cemetery was made of wire and wood. Inside the fence, headstones were scattered about in no particular order. Some were ringed by rusty wrought-iron grilles; some had fallen over; some had been placed there quite recently, and were made of polished granite. No trees were shading the graves, though I could see a few stumps where trees had been chopped down. The grass was coarse and spiky between large patches of brick-hard dirt. I noticed some animal droppings, but I couldn't identify what kind. Sheep droppings, perhaps? Kangaroo pellets?

'*Infant mortality was very high during the Gold Rush era,*' I read aloud, peering at my project sheet. '*Of 129 recorded deaths in Hill End during 1872, no fewer than 74 were those of children. Bronchitis, whooping cough, enteritis, scarlet fever and typhoid fever claimed many victims. How many children's graves can you find in the cemetery, and when did they die?*'

'Cheery,' muttered Michelle. 'Well – here's one. Harold John Egbert, beloved son of Caldwell and Fanny Howard, died November 11th, 1887, aged two years. *He is gone but the flowers that are brightest/ Are culled for the bouquet on high/ And hearts that are purest and lightest/ Are singled to blossom and die.*'

'Oh, dear,' said Mum, and her voice cracked. 'Oh, dear, how sad.'

Michelle and I moved away from her. We began to trudge along purposefully between the headstones, avoiding the hummocks that looked as if they might be unmarked graves. The air was heating up. Beyond the babble of voices, in the watching bush, I sensed an immense and stifling silence.

Glancing over my shoulder, I tracked Jesse down; he was trying to climb the fence around one of the graves. Even as I wondered why a smart boy should feel the urge to do such a thing, I found myself admiring the easy way he swung himself over the wrought-iron spikes. I had to admit, he's quite athletic.

'*Jesse Gerangelos!*' Mrs Patel shouted. '*Get out of there right now!*'

'I wonder if Eustace is buried around here?' Michelle remarked. 'Do you think?'

'Could be.'

'What was his last name?'

'Harrow.'

'Here's another one. *Sacred to the memory of Caroline Henriette Sophie, the beloved daughter of H.C. and Emilie Fischer, who departed this life October 21st AD 1866, aged 11 years, three months and five days.* Gee,' said Michelle, with a shudder. 'That's only a few months younger than me.'

'Look,' I said, and stopped. 'Here's a bunch of Harrows on this stone. Margaret, Thomas, Abel, John and . . . let's see . . . Georgina. No Eustace.'

'It's the wrong date, anyway,' Michelle pointed out. 'The last death shown here happened over a hundred years ago. He can't have died more than eighty-three years ago.'

'Who can't have?' a voice inquired. It was Peter Cresciani, sneaking up on us again.

'No one,' I said shortly.

'Did you see the grave over there?' he continued. 'It belongs to an eight-year-old girl called Frances Deadman. What a great name to have on a gravestone, eh?'

'When did she die?' Michelle asked, and Peter checked his notes.

'March 23rd, 1861,' he declared.

'Thanks,' said Michelle, and scribbled this information down. From the other side of the cemetery, someone – probably Malcolm Morling – began to make ghostly 'ooooing' noises.

'I wondered how long it would take him to do that,' Peter remarked in pensive tones, squinting across the gravestones towards Jesse's gang. It gave me an excuse to do the same. But then I caught Jesse's eye, and glanced away quickly.

'Hey, look,' I said. 'Here are the Ellis graves. There he is – Red Jack Ellis. Died September 24th, 1999, aged eighty-four.'

'And here's another kid,' Peter offered. 'Eustace Harrow, three years – oh no. Hang on. That's too –'

'Where?' I gasped. 'Where is it?'

'Here.' Peter pointed. 'But it's not from the Gold Rush era. This kid died in 1948.'

I jostled him while Michelle jostled me; we were both desperate to look at the gravestone. It wasn't very big. It was made of greyish marble, with inlaid letters forged out of lead. A few of the letters were missing.

'*Sacred to the memory of Eustace Harrow, died 2 April 1948, aged three years,*' Michelle murmured. 'It must be him.'

'It must be who?' asked Peter, and I said: 'No one.' I had noticed that the gravestone beside Eustace's belonged to his mother, Evie (died 6 September 2001, aged eighty-three). Her gravestone was new and glossy, made of black granite, and there were fresh flowers standing in a glass jar right in front of it. Her son's grave, on the other hand, was grubby and weathered. Such a contrast, I thought, was very, very

51

sad. It made me realise how long they had been apart.

No wonder the poor kid was still hanging around –
if that's what he was doing. He had been much too
little to leave his mum.

Then it occurred to me: wouldn't they have been
reunited the minute Evie died?

'Come on,' said Peter. 'We've got to finish this. Can
anyone see any other kids?'

In the end, we collected a lot of kids' names:
Duncan Islay, aged ten years; Elizabeth Ann Gillard,
aged thirteen months; Edgar Paten, aged six weeks;
Louis and Albert Hodge, aged one month and three
years respectively. After a while, this long list began
to depress me even more than Eustace's gravestone.
There seemed to be so many dead kids, stuck out in
the middle of the bush. Some of the fenced graves
began to look like cots, overgrown with weeds.

I was glad when Mrs Patel summoned us back to
the bus.

'Okay – now we're going to visit Golden Gully,'
she said, lurching as the bus hit a rut (or a root) in
the sun-baked surface of the car park. 'A lot of the
old mining activity took place in this area along
Tambaroora Creek. What the miners didn't dig up,
erosion has exposed since then. You'll see a lot of
evidence of the old shafts, but I want you to be *very
careful*, because it's a dangerous area. The ground's
highly unstable. I don't want *anyone* going into any of
those tunnels, is that clear?'

I wondered why she was even putting the idea into Malcolm Morling's head. Michelle said to me: 'Didn't that National Parks woman mention Golden Gully?'

'That's right.' (I pretended to stretch so that I could glance towards the back seat. Jesse was flirting with Amy again.) 'When she was talking about some guy . . .'

'The feral.'

'The fossicker.'

'I wonder if we'll see him today?'

'See who?' asked Peter, who was sitting behind us. 'What feral?'

'Oh, some old bloke who's still panning for gold,' I replied. 'No one special.'

'Is he on the project sheet?'

'Of course not.'

'Then he doesn't matter. Nothing matters unless it's on the project sheet.' As Michelle and I laughed at this, Peter leaned forward. 'How come you guys know all this stuff? Where do you get it from? Why do I feel like you've got crib notes, or something?'

'It's called the project sheet of life, Peter,' I joked, and then we arrived at Golden Gully.

Steve had to park on Tambaroora Road, where he settled down with a newspaper and a cigarette. There was a steep path leading from the dusty little parking area to a small clearing. Behind the clearing, several tall, thin, shaggy eucalypts, as white as bone, framed a low archway that had been weathered into a hillside.

'Right,' said Mrs Patel. 'Gather round, everyone. Tony – come here, please. Golden Gully was what made Tambaroora gold field the biggest attraction in New South Wales in 1852. Originally, it wasn't this deep. What you see now is the result of the earth being riddled with mines, then left to erode. Now, we've already talked about the presence of quartz rock, and how important it is if you're looking for gold. We've also talked about "wash", or gold-bearing gravel. What I want you to do now is divide your-selves into groups, and I'll give you fifteen minutes to go and look for a piece of quartz, a handful of "wash", and one of the circular shafts dug by the Chinese miners. On your project sheet, you'll see that the Chinese miners wouldn't dig oblong shafts because they believed that evil spirits lurked in corners. What is it, Jesse?'

'Please, miss, I think Zoe needs to go to the toilet.'

An explosion of giggles and slaps from the rear of the group. 'I do not!' 'Ow!' 'You think you're *so* funny!'

Mrs Patel, I was pleased to see, didn't take the slightest bit of notice.

'All right,' she said. 'We meet back here in fifteen minutes. If anyone's late, they're in big trouble. And *do not* go anywhere near those shafts. Got that? Okay – off you go.'

I glanced around. Mum was locked in a conversation with Tammy's mother. Angus and Serge were poring over their project sheets. ('*Quartz is a usually colourless transparent crystalline mineral . . .'*) Jesse and his mob were already sprinting down the creek bed, hurrying to escape adult supervision.

I could sympathise with their need for space.

'Come on,' I muttered to Michelle. 'Quick, before Mum catches up.'

'Can I come too?' asked Peter.

'I guess.'

'Gold-bearing gravel,' said Michelle. 'That shouldn't be hard to find.'

We began to follow the winding creek bed, which was mostly dry, though there were patches of flaking mud here and there which still showed traces of moisture between the cracks. On either side, the fretted walls of the gully towered above us, sometimes closing in like nudging shoulders, sometimes opening out into other meandering corridors. The earth really was a golden colour. A hundred and fifty years of wind and rain had carved it into amazing shapes: pinnacles and arches, stalactites and stalagmites. We came to one enormous arch that spanned the whole creek bed, and must have been – I don't know – ten metres high. What's more, there were holes everywhere. Man-sized holes puncturing the walls of the gully, black and deep and yawning like mouths.

'They *all* look round to me,' said Peter. 'At least, they don't look oblong.'

'That hole's got a really curved top, but a flat

bottom,' Michelle observed. Like Peter, she kept her voice low; something in our surroundings made us all want to whisper. 'Do you think it's Chinese, or not?'

'Look,' I breathed. 'Look up there. Don't they look like faces?'

Above our heads loomed strange, sculptured shapes with jutting shelves for chins, shadowy hollows for eyes and crumbling lumps for noses. Not normal noses, mind you. Ogres' noses. Monsters' noses. There were ribbed drums like crowns and drooping tufts of grass-like hair.

'Excellent,' said Peter, in tones of profound satisfaction.

'They remind me of statues in a ruined city,' said Michelle.

'I wish I had a camera,' I remarked, and winced as the shouts and yelps of Jesse's mob reached our ears. Surely Jesse's voice wasn't raised among them? Surely, if left to himself, he would have walked in awe through the brooding landscape, rather than playing the fool for the entertainment of his deadhead companions? 'Don't you hate it when people make so much noise in a place like this?'

'Here's some quartz,' Peter pointed out. Stooping, he picked up a pink-and-white stone from the creek bed. 'At least, I think it's quartz.'

'I don't see what else it could be.' Michelle picked up two more pieces. They glinted in the sunshine. 'One for you, Allie, and one for me.'

'What about the gravel?' Squinting, Peter surveyed the pebbles under his feet. 'Would this do?'

'Let's go a bit further,' I suggested. 'We've still got time.'

Okay, I'll admit it. I wanted to see what Jesse was up to. But no one had a better idea, so we pressed on, beneath the big arch, around a blind corner, past a hole so big that it was practically a cave, and into another stretch of gully where Amy, Tony, Zoe and Malcolm were grouped near one wall, shrieking and laughing and jumping around.

Above them, Jesse's legs were sticking out of a large hole. I could tell they were Jesse's legs, because I had been paying very close attention to everything he wore. The baggy jeans, the football socks, the red-and-black trainers . . .

'Jesse!' I cried, before I could stop myself. 'What are you *doing*?'

Amy turned. 'He's such an idiot,' she simpered at us, in admiring tones.

'Oh, for God's sake.' Peter was clearly disgusted. 'That is so pathetic.'

'Room for one more?' Malcolm Morling yelled. Jesse's feet were waggling about just above his head; Jesse must have climbed up the wall using cracks and lumps as footholds. I couldn't help admiring him for it, because it wasn't an easy climb.

'I said, room for one more?' Malcolm repeated, placing his hands on the edge of the hole and raising one foot to rest in a crevice. Then suddenly Jesse began to kick frantically. His right trainer collided with Malcolm's head.

'*Hey! Hey!*' a muffled voice cried. '*Hey, I'm stuck!*'

'Yeah, right,' said Tony. Malcolm, rubbing his head, growled something unprintable.

'*Help! Help!*'

'Nice try, mate!' Malcolm shouted. Amy and Zoe were laughing excitedly.

Peter turned on his heel. 'Come on,' he said. 'Let's get out of here.'

'No – wait.' I couldn't leave. What if Jesse wasn't playing tricks? What if he really was stuck? How could I walk away if he was in trouble? 'Hang on . . .'

'Grab his feet!' Tony exclaimed, leaping forward. 'Mal! Come on! You pull that one and I'll pull this one.'

'Yeah!' Gleefully, Malcolm obeyed. He began to haul at Jesse's right leg as if it were a piece of rope. Tony did the same with the left leg. It looked painful. I heard someone say '*Ow*'.

'Don't,' I faltered. 'You'll hurt him.'

'*Ow! Stop it!*' The muffled voice was shrill now. '*I can't! Help! Don't!*'

Amy's smile began to fade. This didn't sound like Jesse.

'Stop playing the fool, Gerangelos!' Peter said loudly and sharply, his hands on his hips. 'Don't be an idiot!'

'*I'M STUCK!*'

'You are not!'

'*Somebody help me! Get Mrs Patel!*'

Everyone exchanged glances. My heart skipped a beat.

'Mrs – Mrs Patel?' Malcolm stammered. 'You must be kidding.'

'*GET MRS PATEL!*' Jesse shrieked.

That did it. Amy bolted. Zoe followed her. They rushed past us and disappeared, heading back down the creek. I realised that I had my hands over my mouth.

'He can't be stuck,' Tony muttered, then raised his voice. 'You're not taking the piss, mate? Jess?'

'Of course he is.' Peter approached Jesse's feet. 'Hey! Gerangelos! You can't possibly be stuck! You got in there – you must be able to get out!'

Suddenly the suspended feet gave one convulsive kick; there was a flurry of movement and Jesse's filthy form hit the ground with a thump. He straightened, dusted his clothes and looked around with a big, cheeky grin on his face. 'So,' he said, panting slightly, 'who'd I get rid of? The girls? Good. Come on, you guys – before they get back.'

He wasn't talking to me – or to Michelle. Tony gave a whoop. He and Jesse exchanged a high five.

Malcolm bristled. 'You didn't fool me,' he declared.

'You reckon?'

'You did not!'

'Come on,' said Peter, touching my arm. 'I told you he wasn't stuck.'

'Come on, Allie, we'll be late.'

Jesse didn't ignore us entirely. Before I turned to go (dragging my feet, I have to admit), he shot me a bright, sidelong glance, and touched his forehead in a gesture that was sort of like a salute. Why? For what reason? I couldn't tell. It was like that business of the bikini remark – I didn't know if he was trying to create some kind of *connection* with me, or whether he was just showing off.

Naturally, I hoped that he was singling me out. That salute had made my insides clench up. I thought: maybe he wants me to be *in on the joke*.

Whatever that joke might be.

As we walked away, Peter muttered: 'With any luck, he really *will* get stuck down a mineshaft next time.'

It seemed like a very nasty thing for Peter to be saying. I didn't understand why he had to be so mean.

After all, Jesse had never done *him* any harm.

CHAPTER # five

Michelle, Peter and I retraced our steps. Around us, the air seemed to throb with the pulse of humming flies. (Or was it another insect making that noise? Bees, perhaps?) We passed a tree hung with shiny brown pods. We passed a bush covered in small yellow flowers. A cloud of black-and-orange butterflies rose from a patch of damp mud. As I turned my head to watch them, something else caught my eye.

A movement.

'Look!' I gasped, and stopped.

The others stopped too.

'What?' said Peter.

'Did you see that?'

'See what?'

'That guy!'

'What guy?'

'Didn't you see?'

They shook their heads. I pointed. We were standing at the intersection of two gullies; one of them – smaller and narrower – opened off the great, winding canyon that we were following.

'He was just in there,' I hissed. 'He disappeared around that corner.'

'Must have been Angus's dad,' Peter remarked.

'No! No, he was old! He had white hair!'

'Really?'

'And greyish – sort of greyish clothes.'

Michelle's eyes widened. 'The fossicker?' she suggested.

'The feral?' I frowned. 'Do you think?'

'Are you talking about that gold-panning guy?' asked Peter. When I nodded, he hitched his backpack higher and said: 'Let's go and see. We've still got time.'

'But we have to tell Mrs Patel that Jesse's not stuck,' Michelle pointed out. 'She'll come running up here in a minute.'

'Oh yeah.' We all looked at each other. Then I said to Peter: 'Come on. We'd better go and find Mrs Patel.' To tell you the truth, I wasn't keen to go chasing after that feral. Something about my glimpse of him had made me slightly uneasy.

'But if he's a fossicker,' Peter pointed out, 'he'll be

able to tell us about the gravel.' Seeing our blank faces, he added impatiently: 'The gold-bearing gravel, guys! We still need some.'

'Oh yeah . . .' I'd forgotten about that. 'But isn't it *all* gold-bearing gravel?'

'I don't know. Is it? Maybe this fossicker bloke could tell us.' Without waiting for an answer Peter started to walk away.

I turned to Michelle. 'You'd better find Mrs Patel,' was my suggestion. 'This won't take a minute.'

'What makes you think this bloke is the feral?' she objected. 'He's probably just some tourist.'

'I know. Still – it's worth a try. I guess.'

Michelle shrugged and sighed, and began to trudge back towards the bus. I followed Peter, hurrying along, because I had a feeling that the feral – if he *was* the feral – had been moving very quickly.

Sure enough, when I entered the smaller gully, there was no one else in it except Peter.

'He must have turned the next corner,' I said, and Peter paused to look back at me.

'Will we chase him?'

'I don't know.' I glanced at my watch. 'We've got five minutes.'

'Come on.'

'Well . . . okay.' I was still a bit reluctant. But we pressed forward, and soon the small gully merged into yet another one, wider and deeper, but scrubbier.

Loose slopes of rubble were like foothills propped against the steep peaks of the gully walls. Roots and dead branches were twisted into tortured shapes that were almost painful to see.

'We'd better not get lost,' said Peter.

'What's that noise?'

He stopped and listened. It was the distant sound of screeching voices – the sort of thing you always hear in our school playground.

'It's Jesse being an idiot,' he declared.

'Are you sure?'

'I'm sure.'

We kept going. Small trees and tufts of grass were sprouting from areas where the gully walls were less steep. There were gaping holes everywhere, some high, some low. I had a sudden, chilling thought: what if the old fossicker was hiding in one of those holes, watching us?

'Let's go back,' I said abruptly.

'Are you all right?'

'Of course I am.' I couldn't help flushing, though I was annoyed as well as embarrassed. 'We'll be late, that's all. I don't want to be late.'

Peter shrugged. 'Okay,' he said.

'*You* can stay if you want to. I don't care.'

'*HAAH!*'

It was a shout from behind us, and the shock of it nearly killed me. We whirled around. I dropped my project sheet.

Malcolm Morling came skidding around a corner, covered in dust. He stumbled to a halt when he saw us. 'Oh,' he gasped. 'It's you.'

'Of course it's us, you moron!' Peter cried. His cheeks were red; I could tell that he, too, had been scared. 'What the hell do you think you're doing?'

'I thought – I thought you were Jess and Tones.'

'Well, we're not,' Peter snapped.

I picked up my project sheet.

'Have you seen them?' Malcolm asked.

'Who?' Peter growled.

'Jess and Tones.'

'No, we haven't. Come on, Allie.'

Malcolm's face grew dark. 'They ran away from me!' he spat. 'The rotten sods! They're hiding from me!'

I caught Peter's eye. From his expression, I deduced that the same thought had shot through both our heads at exactly the same time; namely, *I'm not surprised.*

'Where are you going?' Malcolm wanted to know, as we walked past him.

'Where do you think?' I said.

'To the bus?'

'Of course.'

'Then I'll come with you. I'm lost.'

It figured. Peter and I led him back to the little gully that connected the two bigger ones. We were almost out of it when I turned, to check that Malcolm was still behind us.

He was – and so was someone else.

'There!' I shrieked. 'Look!'

The fossicker. He was gone in the blink of an eye, flitting away so quickly that neither of the boys saw him when they swung around. I had an impression of white hair . . . ragged clothes . . . a gaping mouth . . . but it happened so quickly that I couldn't be sure.

'What? What?' Malcolm cried.

'The old guy! He was there!' I yelped.

'Who was?'

'Jeez, Allie!' Peter exclaimed, white-faced. 'You scared the life out of me!'

I pushed past Malcolm and pounded up the gully, following the direction that the old man had chosen to take. But he was gone. There wasn't a trace of him: not a sound, not a footprint, not even a faint smell. The trees and rocks were motionless in the sun.

'*Hey!*' I panted. '*Excuse me! Hey!*'

Nothing.

'Are you sure you saw him?' asked Peter, from behind me. He sounded sceptical.

Behind *him*, Malcolm was waiting for us to return, making plaintive noises. 'What are you *doing?*' he called. 'Come *back!*'

But I ignored him. I had seen the feral, and was determined to prove that I had – that he hadn't been some weird figment of my imagination. The more elusive he became, the more I wanted to pin him down. Just to show that I wasn't going crazy.

'I saw him, Peter. Cross my heart. I really saw him.'

'Where?' Peter demanded. 'Where was he?'

'He went around this corner.' I was trying to catch my breath. My heart was pounding. 'He turned down here.'

'Then where is he now?'

'I don't know.'

'Do you think – do you think he's *hiding*?'

'I don't know.'

We looked at each other, then quickly looked away. Something twisted in my stomach. Around us, the towering walls of the gully waited silently, like sentinels. The air almost seemed to hum.

Peter cleared his throat, his face covered in sweat. 'Let's get out of here,' he said suddenly.

I opened my mouth, but couldn't find the strength to argue. I just said: 'Yes.' All at once, I wanted to get out of the place as much as he did.

We didn't dawdle. After rejoining Malcom, we went straight back to the bus, at a pace that Malcolm found a little brisk, to judge from his protests. On the way, we met up with Mrs Patel. She was looking hot and cross.

'It's all right, Mrs Patel,' I assured her, wondering why Michelle hadn't passed on the news. 'Jesse isn't stuck after all.'

'I know.'

'Then –'

'He's late. I'm going to get him. Who's with him now? Just Tony?'

'Just Tony.'

'All right.' She marched on, breathing heavily, pebbles crunching under her boots. I almost opened my mouth to warn her about the fossicker, but found that I couldn't. I don't know why. Embarrassment, perhaps? Fear?

Instead I returned to the bus in silence, trailing behind Peter and Malcolm. I kept glancing over my shoulder, but I didn't see the old man again. It only occurred to me later that I hadn't been scanning the tops of the gully walls. I still don't know if anyone was up there, watching us over the edge of a crumbling golden cliff.

I could hear Mrs Patel's distant 'Coo-ee!', but nothing else. Nothing else except the insects.

When we arrived at our destination, Mum practically jumped on me.

'Where did you get to?' she demanded. 'I was beginning to worry.'

'We were just collecting quartz, Mum. For our project sheet.'

'You shouldn't wander off like that.'

'I didn't.'

'You did. You're late.'

'I am not!'

'You're two minutes late. Look.' She thrust her watch at me. I saw Peter sidling away, with a sympathetic backward glance. I saw Zoe and Amy giggling together – as if their own mums weren't exactly the same. 'Mrs Patel's gone to look for you, do you know that?'

'She's not looking for me. She's looking for Jesse and Tony. She said so, when we ran into her.'

'Even so, you went much too far.'

'I'm thirsty.'

'The water's in the bus. You can get it yourself.'

She was being unfair, but I decided to forgive her, because it was very hot. I went to the bus and found my water, which I drank in the shade. Soon Michelle joined me; we sat fanning the flies away from our eyes and mouths. The adults were all standing in a group, gazing down the gully from beneath their hands and their hat-brims. The kids were huddled under trees, complaining about ant-bites and sharing around M&Ms.

We waited and waited.

'This is taking too long,' I said at last, glancing at my watch. It was half past twelve. 'She should be back by now. It's lunchtime.'

'Trust Jesse to stuff us all up,' Michelle grumbled. 'I'm starving.'

'So am I.'

'Mum was going to buy us lunch at the Royal Hotel, did you know?'

Michelle groaned. 'Don't tell me that. It only makes things worse. Oh, where *are* they?'

Mum and Tammy's mother (or Esme, as Mum called her) were saying the same thing. They were beginning to get worried. At last Angus's dad suggested that he and Tony's mum should go and see what was wrong; Mum, Tammy's mother and Amy's dad, meanwhile, should look after the rest of us.

But before anyone could do anything, Mrs Patel suddenly appeared. Even from a distance, I could see that she was looking anxious.

I could also see that she was alone.

'Uh-oh,' said Michelle. 'We have a problem.'

'The stupid nong must be lost,' Peter observed, from a patch of shade nearby.

I didn't say anything. I got up and went over to where Mrs Patel was talking to the mums and dads in a quick, sharp, breathless voice. Michelle followed me. So did Peter, Angus and Serge. By the time I could hear what the adults were saying, I was part of a hovering crowd.

'. . . organise a search party.' Mrs Patel had taken her hat off and was running her fingers through her hair. 'Just a small one. To stay here while the rest go back and ring the police.'

'But are you sure?' said Mum. 'Did you call out?'

'Of course I did,' Mrs Patel replied testily. 'There was no response. Nothing.'

'You *lost* them?' Tony's mum exclaimed, in a shrill voice, before Tammy's mum laid a soothing hand on her arm.

'No, no,' she said. 'No one's fault.'

'They're probably hiding,' Angus's dad growled. 'I wouldn't put it past 'em.'

'Oh, they wouldn't.' Mum was shocked. 'Surely they wouldn't be so silly.'

'They wouldn't do that!' Tony's mum cried, rounding on Angus's dad. 'You talk about your own son!'

'Shh. It's all right, Mrs Karavias,' said Mrs Patel. And then Mum caught sight of my face.

'What is it, Allie?' she demanded.

Everyone looked at me. I felt hot all over.

'I – I think I . . .' It was so hard to get the words out. 'I might've . . . uh . . . seen someone,' I finished lamely. At which point all the adults fired questions at me.

'What do you mean?'

'Saw whom?'

'When?'

'Where?'

'You mean Jesse? You saw Jesse?'

'No,' I mumbled. Glancing at Michelle, I noticed that she was biting her lip, while Peter stared at the ground. 'It was an old man in the gully. Up there.' I pointed.

'A tourist?' said Mrs Patel.

'I don't know. I – I don't think so.' As they stared at me, I added desperately: 'His clothes weren't right. They were sort of . . . strange.'

'Strange?' This time it was Amy's dad talking. 'In what way?'

'Well . . . it was like he hadn't taken them off or washed them in about a hundred years.'

There was a long silence. The adults stopped looking at me and glanced at each other.

'Okay.' Angus's dad suddenly spoke up, briskly and firmly. 'Victor – you and I can stay with Mrs Patel. We'll start searching. Judy, you and the other mothers take the kids back to town. You'd better talk to the police when you get there.'

'No!' Tony's mum objected. 'I have to stay! He's my son!'

'He's her son, Bob,' Amy's dad pointed out. 'I mean, if she wants to stay . . .'

'Hang on a minute,' Mum interrupted. 'I've got a mobile. We can ring the police from here.'

So that's what they did. Mrs Patel called the Hill End police, who agreed to send someone out as soon as possible. Meanwhile, a National Parks and Wildlife Officer would be coming to help us.

'Apparently he knows his way around this area,' Mrs Patel declared, as she handed the mobile back to my mum. 'He knows where all the dangerous shafts are.'

'What do you mean?' Tony's mother shrilled. 'What's dangerous?'

'It's all right, Mrs Karavias,' said Mum. 'I'm sure Tony hasn't fallen down any holes.'

'I'll find him.' Tony's mum raised her voice. *'Tony! TONY!'*

'Wait.' Amy's dad put a hand on her shoulder. 'Hang on. Let's do this properly. We should divide into groups, and leave one group here, to wait for this Parks guy –'

'Not the kids,' Mrs Patel broke in firmly. 'I'm not having any more kids wandering around out there. The kids can go back to Hill End. They haven't eaten yet.'

'But who's going to go with them?' Amy's dad asked.

'And what about Malcolm?' Angus's dad wanted to know. 'He was the last to see those two boys – we'll need him to show us where.'

In the end, it was decided that Amy's dad would take most of the kids back to Hill End in the bus. Mrs Patel would wait for the National Parks and Wildlife Officer near the road. Malcolm would show Tony's mum and Angus's dad where he had last seen Jesse and Tony. And I would show Mum and Tammy's mother where I had last seen the white-haired old man.

'Just on the off-chance,' Mrs Patel said cagily, without going on to explain herself. But I knew what she was thinking. She was thinking that maybe the feral might have had something to do with Jesse's disappearance.

'Here,' said Michelle, handing me her last almond bar. 'Since you're obviously not going to be eating for a while.'

'Mum says there's bread and tomatoes and cheese sticks in the tent, but no butter,' I sighed. 'She says to help yourself.'

'Are we going back to the camping ground?'

'I don't know.'

'I thought we were going to History Hill.'

'You'd better ask Amy's dad.'

'I bet Jesse's just playing up,' Michelle concluded, trying to reassure me. She patted my back, her eyebrows knotted into an expression of sympathetic concern. 'Are you going to be all right?'

'I guess.'

'It seems pretty stupid that *I* can't stay.'

'We could ask.'

'I already did. Mrs Patel said no.' Michelle shook her head, sighing. 'It seems so stupid.'

Then she got on the bus with everyone else. I was so anxious and confused that I forgot to wave goodbye when the bus drove off. I still feel mean about that.

'Here,' said Mrs Patel, handing Mum her whistle. 'If you find anything, give two sharp blasts.'

'What about us?' Angus's dad frowned. 'What'll we do?'

'Send someone back.'

'If only there was another mobile,' Mum said regretfully, 'we could keep in touch by phone.'

I glanced at Malcolm Morling. He was looking bewildered. For once I could sympathise; I was still in a state of shock myself. One half of me was frightened. The other half felt that perhaps the adults were over-reacting, because Jesse couldn't really be lost. As Michelle had said, he was probably just playing up.

But I didn't say this out loud, of course. It wouldn't have been the right moment.

'So,' Mum said to me with an unconvincing smile. 'Are we all ready?'

'I guess.'

'Mrs Patel wants us to check the area where you saw the old man. Do you remember where that was?'

'Yeah.' All too well.

'Right. Where's Esme? Oh – there you are. All set? Yes? Good.' Mum took a deep breath. 'Okay,' she said brightly. 'Let's go then.'

CHAPTER # six

'*Jesse!*'

'*Tony!*'

'*Jesse, where are you?*'

Tammy's mother had a very small, thin shout – perhaps because she was so small and thin herself. Looking at her, I decided that Bethan would have fitted quite nicely into her jeans, except that he never would have worn jeans with a spotted dog embroidered on the back pocket. Tammy's mother also wore the whitest T-shirt I've ever seen and a tiny pair of pink-and-white sneakers that still looked big and chunky on the ends of her spindly ankles.

She seemed out of place in the bush – too neat and clean.

Mum, on the other hand, was sweating like a pig.

'Down here?' she asked, pointing, and I nodded. We advanced cautiously into the short gully where I had last seen my feral. Ahead, around the next corner, something cast a shadow over the dry creek bed – something hunched and bulky, with waving arms.

When we reached it, we found a rock poised on the edge of the gully wall, with a couple of young trees growing out of it. The trees were dancing in the breeze that had started to blow.

'I was supposed to drop in on Samantha after lunch,' Mum suddenly remarked. 'To meet up with Richard and Delora.'

'Oh, yeah.' I had forgotten Richard and Delora. 'When are they supposed to arrive?'

'About now.'

'Oh.'

'If Samantha had a phone, I could ring and explain.'

'Doesn't Richard have a mobile?'

'If he does, I don't know the number. Right or left, Allie?'

'Right.'

We kept walking. With every step we took, a new stretch of creek bed opened out before us. The wind was rushing through the treetops far overhead, making a noise like the sea, but down in the gully we could hardly feel it except as a teasing breath on the back of our necks. Passing a hole in the gully wall, I slowed reluctantly.

'Mum?'

'What?'

'I was thinking . . . when we were here, me and Peter . . .' I swallowed. 'I wondered if he might be hiding in one of these holes . . .'

'Who? Jesse?'

'The old guy.'

She blinked at me, her forehead puckering, then glanced quickly at the hole. It yawned ominously.

'Oh, no,' she said, sounding shaken. 'It's too small.'

'Yeah. But there are bigger ones.'

'Why would he have been hiding?'

'I don't know.'

'You mustn't let this place get to you, Allie. I realise it has a strange energy signature, but that doesn't necessarily mean much.'

'Judy! Look!'

It was Tammy's mother. She had picked up a folded piece of white paper, which had been fluttering down a kind of path or shallow incline that you could climb if you wanted to get out of the gully. Standing at the top of this incline, she waved the piece of paper at us.

'Come here!' she exclaimed.

'What is it?' Mum inquired, raising her voice.

'I think maybe Jesse's project sheet, do you think?'

Mum and I quickly scrambled up the slope to see. Sure enough, the piece of paper had Jesse's name on it. Otherwise, it was unmarked except for a date – 1870 – scribbled after one of the questions.

Obviously Jesse hadn't been doing much work.

'Oh, my God,' Mum breathed and gazed around her. '*Jesse?*' she yelled. '*JESSE!*' But there was nothing to see – only scrubby bush, spiky grass, dead trees and the gaps in the ground where the gullies were.

'Mum?' I couldn't stop my voice from trembling. 'He'll be all right, won't he?'

'*JESSE?* Of course he will. *JESSE!*'

'The paper was blowing down,' said Tammy's mother. 'Down from here. I saw.'

'Did the old man come up here?' Mum asked me.

'No. I don't know.' I could hardly think, I was so worried about Jesse. Where *was* he? 'Where *are* they, Mum?'

'Shh!' Tammy's mother raised her hand. 'Listen.'

We listened. All I could hear was leaves swishing.

'What?' Mum whispered. 'What is it?'

'Someone's voice, I thought.'

We listened again. The wind died down for a moment. Then I heard it too.

'Probably just Ted and Maria,' Mum began.

'No! Shh!' Tammy's mother flapped her hands wildly. 'Listen!'

'There!' I caught my breath. 'It's – it's –'

'From that way,' said Tammy's mum.

Mum and I strained to catch the thread of sound. Another gust of wind drowned it out, but we heard it again when the wind died.

'There!' I squeaked.

'What – I mean, can you tell –?' Mum stammered.

'"Help,"' Tammy's mother breathed. She stared at us, her eyes wide with distress. 'Is that what it is?'

'Oh, no,' I whimpered.

'*JESSE!*' Mum screamed. '*TONY! WHERE ARE YOU?*'

This time there could be no doubt. A faint, muffled voice cried, '*Here!*' I clutched Mum's arm.

'That way! It's that way!'

'Come on,' she gasped.

'*Jesse!*' I screamed, but she flung out a hand, as if to check me.

'No. Don't shout. We have to listen.'

It was hard because the ground was all snapping sticks and crunching grass. We couldn't help grunting, either, as we scrambled over fallen trees and pushed clawing dead branches out of our way. Sometimes we had to stop in our tracks, all of us, and listen. Then we could hear the voice again, cracking as it pleaded for help.

'*Here! I'm here! Hurry!*'

'Is it Jesse or Tony?' Mum demanded, her fingers digging into my neck. 'Can you tell?'

'I – I don't know.' Never having heard either of them in a genuine state of panic, I couldn't be sure. And it occurred to me that there was one other possibility.

'Mum,' I said, catching at her sleeve before she could move forward. 'You don't think – I mean . . .'

'What?' She waited. But I couldn't say it out loud. I couldn't say: 'What if it's the old man, trying to lure us into a trap?' The whole notion was ridiculous. I knew

80

that. Especially since my mother had never seen him –
had never felt that weird sense of being watched . . .

'Nothing,' I mumbled.

'Come on! We're so close!'

We were, in fact, very close. We didn't realise how
close until Tammy's mother, with a little shriek, nearly
fell down a hole. It wasn't a gully – it was an honest-
to-goodness mineshaft, overgrown with weeds and
lined with a couple of rotting wooden boards. It was
small, it was dark, and it was extremely dangerous.

'*Here! I'm here!*' cried the voice, from the bottom of it.

'Oh, my God,' Mum squeaked.

'Jesse?' Tammy's mother cried. 'Is that you?'

'*Yes! It's me! Get me out! Get me OUT!*' He was practically
howling. He sounded so strange. Again, I thought of
my silly idea about the old man, lurking in holes,
watching . . .

'Where's Tony?' Mum shouted. 'Is he down there too?'

'*Yes! He's down here! He's hurt!*'

'Oh, my God,' Mum repeated. She was beginning
to panic; I could tell.

'Mum, blow the whistle,' I urged. 'Quick, blow it.'

'Oh! Oh, yes!' She groped down the front of her
shirt, pulled Mrs Patel's whistle out, fumbled, dropped
it, then put it to her lips and blew.

The noise was piercing.

'It's all right, Jesse!' she yelled. 'Help is on the way!
Allie.' She lowered her voice. 'Go and tell Mrs Patel,
will you? Quickly!'

'Who, me? No way.' I wasn't about to return alone. I wasn't about to leave Jesse – or Mum.

'But Allie, she mightn't have heard the whistle.'

'Then blow it again.'

'I will go,' said Tammy's mother. 'I will go now.'

'Hey! Don't go! Are you still there?'

'It's all right, Jesse!' Mum bellowed, before smiling gratefully at Tammy's mother. 'We won't leave you! Esme, are you sure you can find the right path?'

'Oh, yes. No problem.'

Tammy's mother hurried away, so light on her feet that the dry sticks barely cracked beneath her shock-proof soles. We watched her go, and I felt a bit ashamed of myself, but I couldn't help it. The very thought of leaving made my stomach lurch. To be walking around on my own, with a feral on the prowl . . . Besides, I couldn't abandon Jesse.

'It wasn't my fault!' he was saying, his voice hoarse with emotion. *'We weren't being stupid! We were chased!'*

'It's all right, Jesse.' Mum was trying to soothe him, without much success; her own voice was shaking. 'Can Tony talk? How is he? What happened to him?'

'We were digging,' Jesse continued, as if he hadn't heard, *'and my hand got stuck in the dirt! I couldn't pull it out! And then I looked up, and he was there! This old man! He hissed at me! He – he had no eyes!'* Jesse sounded frantic. *'There were no eyes, but he was coming for me!'*

'Oh, my God,' I breathed, casting a quick glance around. But there was no one lurking nearby.

'Calm down,' said Mum. 'Jesse? We're here. Please – tell me about Tony. Can he talk?'

'I pulled my hand out, and I ran! We both did – me and Tony – but he chased us into a cliff! We had to climb up! He grabbed my foot . . .' Jesse's wail broke on a sob. It was weird. I thought: that isn't Jesse. That can't be Jesse – not the Jesse I know. And something cold clutched at my heart. *'But I got away, and we climbed up, and we ran, and we fell!'* the high-pitched voice continued. *'He chased us right in here!'*

'Jesse, *I need to know about Tony!'* Mum shouted. 'What's wrong with him?'

There was a mumbled reply. Mum and I looked at each other. Her face was contorted with anxiety and fear.

'What's that?' she bawled. 'Jesse? What did you say?'

'I didn't say anything! It was Tony!' Jesse seemed a little calmer, though still very shaken. *'He can't yell, because it hurts him to breathe!'*

'Dear God,' Mum moaned.

'His leg hurts too,' Jesse went on. *'And his hand!'*

'Mum,' I whispered. 'Is he going to be all right?'

'I'm sure he is. I'm sure he will be.' Suddenly Mum cocked her head, and sucked in her breath. 'What's that?' she hissed.

It was Mrs Patel; I recognised her voice instantly. I couldn't see her, but I could hear her. The sound of her panted complaint – 'I can't believe they could be so stupid, when I specifically warned them' – seemed to float on the air, and I realised that she must be down in the nearest gully.

'Mrs Patel?' I called.

'*Allie?*' she replied. '*Is that you?*'

'We're up here!'

Mum blew her whistle again, just for good measure. Within five minutes, Mrs Patel was climbing over the edge of the gully wall. Behind her were Tammy's mother and two strange men – one of them wearing a National Parks and Wildlife uniform. The other, I noticed, was carrying a gym bag.

'They've fallen down a mine shaft,' Mum gabbled. 'They're down there – Tony's hurt –'

'I know,' Mrs Patel interrupted. 'Esme told us.' Her skin looked grey. 'What's wrong with him?'

'It hurts when he breathes. His leg hurts too, and his hand –'

'Get away from that edge,' the National Parks officer said sharply. Mrs Patel pulled back, just as sharply, and the National Parks officer apologised. 'It's probably unstable,' he explained. 'We don't want anyone else falling down there.'

'You should have put a fence up!' Mrs Patel snapped. 'Why isn't there a fence?'

'We can't put a fence around every hole in this area,' the National Parks officer rejoined (quite calmly, I thought). The name-badge on his chest said *Ron Gorridge*. 'We put signs up. We expect people to read 'em.'

'There used to be a fence here. Look.' I pointed to the rusty strands of barbed wire sticking out of a bush. Then the other man – the man with the gym bag – said in low, rough, growling tones, 'Let's not stand around yakkin', eh?' and began to pull things out of his gym bag. A nylon rope. A trowel. A bunch of long, metal pegs and spikes that clinked as they fell on top of each other.

'Right,' Ron Gorridge agreed. He put a hand to his sunburned forehead. He was one of those men with very hairy arms and legs, blond but hairy. He wore a big, shady hat. 'Sounds like we need to call an ambulance, first off.'

'Oh – oh, I can do that,' Mum offered, practically putting up her hand. 'But I think you should know – Jesse told me – he was chased.'

Everyone turned to look at her.

'What?' said Ron.

'Jesse and Tony – some old man chased them, and they fell in. That's what Jesse says.'

'What old man?' Ron scowled.

'I don't know.'

'He had no eyes,' I squeaked, and it was my turn to be stared at.

'What do you mean?' asked Ron. 'Who didn't?'

'The old man.' I cleared my throat. 'He – he had no eyes.'

'If he had no eyes, then how could he chase anyone?' Ron drawled, and his friend with the rough voice said: 'Old Abel Harrow's missin' one eye.'

They blinked at each other. Mum gave me a nudge. Mrs Patel said: 'What's wrong, Allie?'

'N-nothing.'

'You jumped.'

'It's okay.' The name 'Harrow' had come as a shock to me – and to Mum too, I suppose – because of Eustace. But no one pressed me for an explanation. The whole group was too busy listening to Ron.

'Nah,' he said slowly. 'Old Abel? Nah. He couldn't have.'

'All I'm sayin' is, Abel's lost his left eye,' Ron's friend pointed out.

'You mean his right eye.'

'His left.'

'Excuse me,' Mrs Patel interjected, 'but we have an injured boy down there. We must get him out, if you don't mind!'

Ron's friend squinted at her without speaking. Ron introduced him as Vern, who had come to help. 'But only if the boys can be moved,' he added, and leaned towards the gaping black mouth of the mineshaft. 'What are their names again? Jesse and . . .?'

'Tony,' Mrs Patel supplied.

'*Jesse? Can you hear me?*' Ron yelled.

'*Yes!*' came the quavering answer.

'*Jesse, I'm Officer Gorridge, from National Parks and Wildlife! Are you hurt, down there?*'

A pause. Then: *'I scraped all the skin off my knees and my hands!'*

I winced, and heard Mum groan. Ron clicked his tongue.

'Can you move?' he shouted.

'Yes!'

'Can you walk?'

'Yes!'

'If someone came down there to help you, could you climb up a rope?'

'I – I think so.' Jesse's voice suddenly became shrill. *'But what about Tony?'*

'We'll sort Tony out, don't worry about it!' Ron turned back to address the rest of us, all at once very brisk. 'Okay,' he said. 'Vern's going to fix things up down there. I'll put a call though to the local volunteer ambulance service, and they'll be able to stabilise this kid until the ambulance unit arrives from base, whenever that might be. Did you say there were some other people wandering around out here?' He was talking to Mrs Patel, who seemed to bristle at his tone.

'They are looking for the lost boys,' she began, but was cut short.

'Well, you'd better go and make sure *they* haven't fallen down any holes,' said Ron. 'And for God's sake don't go on your own.'

'But I must stay!' Mrs Patel protested. 'The boys . . . it's my responsibility . . .' Tammy's mother, however, laid a hand on her arm.

'What about Mrs Karavias?' she said haltingly. 'We must tell her.'

'Oh. Yes.' Mrs Patel looked embarrassed. 'Of course.' She took a deep breath. 'If you come with me, Esme, we'll go and find Maria. Judy, you'd better take Allie back to the car, okay? It's not good for her to be here.'

'Car?' said Mum. 'What car?'

'It's my four-wheel drive,' Ron remarked, butting in. 'It's up on the road, in that little parking bay, you know where that is?' Mum nodded. 'It's not locked,' he finished. 'You'll be fine in there.'

'But my phone,' Mum objected. 'Won't you need my phone?'

'Got one,' Ron replied shortly. 'What do you reckon, Vern? Is it manageable?'

He was definitely in charge; no one wanted to argue. So as he and Vern began to discuss ropes and friction and load-bearing ratios, Mum and I set off for his car, with Tammy's mother and Mrs Patel trailing behind us. We soon parted ways. The other two went upstream to look for poor Mrs Karavias; Mum and I went downstream to look for Ron Gorridge's car.

We found it without any trouble. It was a greeny-yellow colour, and marked with the National Parks and Wildlife Service logo.

We both got into the back seat.

'I can't believe this,' said Mum. She sounded immensely tired. Her face was smudged, her clothes were dusty. 'I can't believe this is happening.'

I had nothing to say. It was all bottled up inside. Abel Harrow? Who *was* this Abel Harrow? Evie's brother? Her husband? Her *son*? Could one of Evie's relations be the feral with the white hair?

Surely not.

As for Jesse – well, I couldn't face the thought of him at all. Not at all. Something funny had happened there.

'You should never have been allowed to wander off on your own in the first place,' Mum went on. 'Mrs Patel should never have let you all do it.'

'Don't blame Mrs Patel,' I responded wearily. 'It wasn't her fault that Jesse got chased.'

'He never would have been chased if he hadn't been out wandering around by himself.'

'He wasn't by himself. He was with Tony.'

'You know what I mean.'

We fell silent. My stomach growled. I took Michelle's almond bar out of my pocket, unwrapped it, and ate it.

If you're wondering what I was thinking, the answer is: nothing much. I was suddenly very tired, and my mind didn't seem to be working properly.

'Samantha and the others must be wondering what's happened to us,' Mum observed, after a while. 'If only I knew Richard's mobile number!'

More time passed. We waited and waited. I offered Mum a bite of my almond bar, but she declined. We drank the last of her water. Then it occurred to me: my project sheet!

'My project sheet! Where's my project sheet?'

'Is it in your pocket?'

I checked. 'No.'

'What about your back pocket?'

'It's not there either!'

'Well, calm down, Allie, I'll look in my bag. I seem to remember putting something in there.'

'That was *Jessie's* project sheet!' I don't know why I was so upset, but I was. 'Oh *no*! I've *lost* it!'

'You couldn't have lost it. Ron Gorridge wouldn't let you lose it – it would spoil the environment. Hang on. Let me look in here . . .'

A tap on the window glass made us both scream. We'd been so busy peering into Mum's bag that we hadn't seen Angus's dad approaching us. Malcolm was with him.

'It's all right,' Angus's dad said gruffly. 'It's only me.'

'What's happening?' Mum asked, as he climbed into the front seat, jangling keys. Malcolm slid into the seat beside him. 'What are you doing?'

'I've been told to drive you all to town and fetch the district nurse. Apparently she's on duty at the clinic from two to three, so I should be able to get hold of her.'

'Why? Is it bad?' Mum exclaimed. Angus's dad turned Ron's key in the ignition, and started pushing the gear stick about.

'I don't know,' he replied curtly. 'I do what I'm told. That Parks guy just thought of this community nurse, so off I went. At least she'll have a first-aid box, or something.'

With a lurch and a bump, the four-wheel-drive moved onto the road, churning up dust. Then Angus's dad hauled at the steering wheel, and we did a U-turn. We were heading back to Hill End.

We didn't actually pass the cemetery; it was further down the road. But something about the dirt tracks leading into the bush on our left made me think of the iron grilles, the brick fence and the gravestones.

And then I remembered.

Abel Harrow?

That was the name on one of the gravestones in the Tambaroora cemetery.

CHAPTER # seven

'It can't *be* the same guy,' said Michelle. 'They must be relatives – him and the dead Abel.'

'Maybe.' That was certainly possible; I had to admit it. 'Or maybe not.'

'Allie, he can't be a ghost,' Michelle insisted. 'He can't be dead, or people would know. It doesn't make sense.'

'It might,' I said slowly, 'if everyone *does* think he's some sort of relative – if everyone just takes him for granted, without stopping to think how old he might be, or where he might come from. He's a feral, after all. He's supposed to live in the bush. No one seems to know anything about him.'

Michelle appeared to be struck by this argument. She thought about it as I finished my cheese and biscuits. We were sitting by our tent in the Village

Camping Area, where Mum and I had been dropped not twenty minutes before. Since then, Mum had been talking furiously with Amy's dad, while I told Michelle about the latest developments.

'It seems like an awful lot of ghosts,' Michelle finally objected. 'First the matron, then Eustace and now Abel. What are the chances?'

'In a town like this?' I shrugged. 'If you ask me, the chances are pretty high.'

'I suppose Abel was *behaving* a bit like a ghost,' Michelle had to agree. 'Appearing and disappearing.'

'Chasing Jesse.'

'You really think he chased Jesse and Tony into that hole?'

'Either that or they got freaked. *I* got freaked.' Shaking my head, I wrapped my arms around myself. 'It's spooky, that place. Golden Gully.'

'But why chase them? Eglantine never chased anyone.'

'She didn't need to. She had other ways of scaring people.' After pondering this for a while, I added: 'Not that she particularly wanted to scare people. She just wanted to get her book finished.'

'So if Abel's a ghost, what does he want? To kill people? What good is that going to do him?'

I shivered.

'Don't say that,' I mumbled. 'Those boys aren't dead.'

'How are they?'

'I don't know. Jesse could talk, at least. Tony didn't seem so good.'

'Poor Tony.'

'Poor Mrs Karavias.'

'I wonder if we'll have to go home?'

It was a good question. So far we'd already missed our visit to History Hill, which had been scheduled for two o'clock. Everybody was sitting huddled together in little groups, glumly eating a late lunch. With Jesse and Tony missing, the spark seemed to have gone out of us all. Even Malcolm was pale and subdued. When asked if he had seen Jesse being pulled out of the old mineshaft, he had shaken his head.

'They were still messing around with the rope,' he'd muttered. 'They made me leave.'

'So you didn't see anything?' I'd pressed him.

'No.'

'Did you see the old man?'

'No.'

'Did you notice anything else weird?'

'Look, just leave me alone, will you?!'

And that was all I had managed to get out of Malcolm. But I didn't blame him. I didn't want to talk or even think about the mineshaft myself – the mineshaft, Jesse, Tony or Abel. The emotion surrounding that concealed hole had been so raw. Jesse's voice had been so frightening. And though I had come to accept that the voice I'd heard floating up out of the dark *had* been Jesse's, in my heart of hearts I couldn't help believing that it had belonged to an entirely different boy. Not to the boy with the cheeky grin who had once drawn a still-life of dog poo for his art project.

No, the desperate boy down the mineshaft had been someone else entirely. Someone in whom I wasn't the slightest bit interested. Someone who was part of something dark and nasty and frightening and . . . and *real*. Frighteningly real.

'Perhaps Abel doesn't actually want to *kill* anyone,' Michelle suddenly suggested. 'Perhaps he just wants to scare them away from Golden Gully, do you think?'

'Perhaps,' I sighed.

'Like a dog guarding his territory. That would make sense. Oh!' Michelle swung around to face me. 'What if he's guarding a *treasure*? What if he has a whole lot of gold down there somewhere, and doesn't want anyone finding it?'

That didn't sound right to me. 'How do you mean?' I said. 'What kind of gold?'

'Gold that he's mined.'

'Ghosts can't dig for gold.'

'How do you know?'

I had to confess that I didn't, not for sure. 'But it's more likely to be gold that he found when he was alive. Though even then . . .' It still didn't feel right, somehow. 'Why didn't he take it to the mining registrar, and sell it?'

'Maybe he died before he could do that.'

'I suppose.'

'Maybe that's why he haunts the place. Because he can't bear to leave his gold.'

'Maybe.'

Then Mum approached us, eating an apple and looking exhausted. She said that she wanted to find out if Richard had arrived at Samantha's place. Would Michelle and I mind popping up there, and making inquiries? 'I can't leave Victor with all these kids,' she said. 'It wouldn't be fair. And I know you two girls are reliable.'

'But, Mu-um . . .'

'Please, Allie. Please. Samantha and Richard have to know what's happened, and I can't call them. I don't have their number. Be nice.'

It was impossible to refuse. Grudgingly I agreed to make things easier for Mum, and began to trudge up the road with Michelle at my side. As we dodged the bigger potholes and flapped the flies away, Michelle suddenly suggested that we tell Richard about Abel.

'We could ask him about the gold,' she said. 'We could ask him what he thinks.'

'Oh, no,' I groaned. 'Don't let's.'

'Why not? He'd be interested, wouldn't he?'

'Yes, but it's all too horrible,' I protested. 'It's not like Eglantine. You weren't there when we found Jesse. You didn't see it.'

'I saw enough,' Michelle replied, sounding slightly offended. 'Anyway, if Abel's a ghost, and he's chasing kids into holes, don't you think something should be done to stop him? *I* certainly do.'

She was right, of course. We had to do something. I was still wondering what that something might be when we arrived at Taylor's cottage, and saw that a little silver hatchback was parked next to Samantha's battered red car. I recognised the PRISM sticker on the hatchback's rear window.

Obviously, Richard Boyer had arrived.

'He's here,' I said.

'Good,' said Michelle.

'Maybe they'll give us some food,' I muttered. 'Are you starving? I am. Those cheese and biscuits weren't enough.' We walked up the front path, between enormous lavender bushes, and I tugged at the cast-iron bell-pull near a door that had 'Welcome' painted on it. We could hear someone approaching from the back of the house, because the floors creaked so much. It turned out to be Samantha.

'Hello!' she exclaimed. 'We'd almost given up on you!'

'Mum couldn't come, because something happened,' I announced. 'She sent me to make sure Richard's all right.'

'Of course! Come in! He's out the back with Delora, waving his machine around.' Samantha giggled. 'It's all so exciting.'

Michelle gave me a nudge – I don't know why. Then we followed Samantha down the dingy hall, through the kitchen and into the garden again. Here, among patches of tomato plants and runner beans, we found Richard peering into the outdoor dunny, clutching an electromagnetic field detector. In some ways he looked the same as ever: pale and thin, with bright blue eyes and curly hair. But instead of his usual rimless spectacles, plain red jumper and baggy jeans, he was wearing sunglasses, a white jacket and shiny grey pants so narrow that his legs looked like pipe-cleaners.

I decided that Delora must have been buying him clothes.

'Hello, Allie, who's this?' he said, in his quick, breathless voice.

'This is my friend Michelle.' I looked around. 'Where's Delora?'

'Down there.' He pointed. 'She's getting a feel for the place. She needs to be alone.'

Shading my eyes, I saw that Delora was way down at the bottom of the garden, where a collapsing post-and-rail fence separated Samantha's land from a great big patch of blackberries. Delora's hair was now a kind of purplish red, instead of blonde, but I couldn't tell if she was wearing her pink leather pants. There was a kiln in the way.

'Has she sensed anything?' I inquired, and Richard shrugged.

'I don't know,' he answered. 'She hasn't said. *I* certainly haven't.'

'No?'

'Nothing exceptional.' He turned to Samantha. 'High volumes of electromagnetic activity are usually associated with reports of apparitions. But I can't see any anomalies in the readings I'm getting.'

Samantha treated us to one of her nervous little laughs. 'I never knew technology had advanced so far!' she twittered. 'Imagine being able to scan for ghosts!'

'It's not foolproof,' Richard admitted, 'but it's very useful.' Gazing around, he added: 'It doesn't feel right. Do you know what I mean, Allie? Your house *felt* different when Eglantine was there.'

I understood exactly what he was saying. Taylor's cottage seemed to be sinking into the ground behind a sunlit screen of herbs and daisies and climbing roses, like a cat drowsing in a bush of catnip. Bees hummed. Birds twittered. Everything looked warm and sleepy and contented.

As Richard had said, it didn't feel right.

'What I'll do tonight, though, is set up my cameras and see if we can spot anything,' he went on, turning back to Samantha. 'Did you say that things only get broken or rearranged when you're out of the house, is that right?'

'That's right,' said Samantha, blinking.

'Then maybe you and Hessel could pop out for a couple of hours, when it gets dark. Just in case Eustace is a bit shy. Would that be okay?'

Samantha said that she supposed it would be. She said that she and Hessel could always go to the pub. Or maybe they could have dinner with Judy, at the camp site. How did that sound?

The question was aimed at me. I didn't know how to respond to it.

'Things are pretty weird down there, right now,' I said at last. 'Maybe . . . that is, I don't even know how long we're going to be here . . .'

'What do you mean?' The lines around Samantha's eyes became deeper and darker. 'I thought you weren't leaving until tomorrow?'

'It all depends . . .'

'On what?'

I had to explain. I told them about Jesse and Tony and the mineshaft. When I got to the bit about Jesse blaming Abel, Samantha began to squeak and gasp.

'I've *heard* about him!' she cried. 'Somebody mentioned him the other day, at the pub! He's supposed to be a prospector, isn't he? Or released from a mental hospital, someone said. One of those hopeless cases . . . comes and goes . . . never talks to anyone . . . bad tempered, but basically harmless. That's what they said. Oh, my God!' She shuddered. 'How *awful*! But it might have been a misunderstanding, don't you think?'

I shrugged. Richard pushed his glasses up his nose.

'Oh, dear,' he said. 'Is your mother all right, Allie?'

'She's fine. But she had to stay with the other kids. That's why she couldn't come.'

'What's happening? Have they called the police?'

More explanations. This time, however, Michelle joined in. I was talking about the ambulance, and the district nurse, and Officer Gorridge, when she suddenly blurted out: 'We think Abel Harrow might be a ghost.'

I shot her the dirtiest of all my dirty looks.

'A ghost?' Richard echoed, and Samantha giggled.

'Because Abel Harrow's name is on a gravestone in the cemetery,' Michelle continued. She was beginning to lose courage; I could tell.

'But there might have been more than one Abel Harrow,' Richard pointed out gently. 'Names do run in families, you know.'

'Evie must have been a relative,' Samantha butted in. 'Her name was Harrow. Do you remember, Richard? Evie used to live in this house.'

'Yes, but he had no eyes!' Michelle gabbled desperately, ignoring Samantha. Richard was the one she wanted to convince. 'Jesse said that the old man had no eyes! He must have been a ghost. And Allie saw him too – she says he was really weird, there one minute and gone the next. Didn't you, Allie?'

I couldn't deny it. I mumbled something, scratching my cheek.

'Did you notice his eyes?' Richard asked me. 'When you saw him?'

'No.'

'Did he look strange to you?'

I cleared my throat. 'Sort of,' I muttered. 'He . . . he . . .'

'What?'

'He moved so *fast*!' (How had he managed to stay out of sight, when Peter and I turned that corner?) 'Unless he was hiding in holes, or something. I thought he might be hiding in the old mine-shafts.'

'Which is creepy enough in itself,' Delora piped up, from behind me. I nearly had a heart attack; no one had noticed her approach. 'Hello, Allie, poor baby, give me a kiss,' she squawked, and left her lipstick on my cheek. The lipstick was a very, very dark red – almost purple. She was also wearing a fluffy lime-green jacket, black lycra pants, snake-skin boots with high heels, and a ring in her belly button. The skin on her face was even more leathery than Samantha's. 'So you've found us another ghost, have you?' she went on, gazing into my eyes. 'It doesn't surprise me. I said to Richard, when I first saw you, that girl has the darkest aura I've ever seen. She's a troubleshooter. She's *special*.' Turning to Michelle, Delora added, 'Hello, sweetie, what's your name?'

'Michelle.'

'I'm Delora. That's a gorgeous bracelet. Real gold? Yes, I thought so.'

'It's my mum's.'

'Gorgeous,' Delora repeated. 'Mind if I have a smoke out here, Sam? That won't bother you, will it?'

'Well – no-o-o . . .'

'I'm *dying* for a ciggie. Takes it out of you, opening yourself up like that. Leaves you so drained.' She began to feel around in her purse, without pausing for breath. 'Not that it did any good, mind you. Pointless. A pointless exercise. Can't feel a thing.'

'No disruptions?' Richard asked, leaning forward.

'Not a thing. Zilch. Inside and out, the whole place. Not so much as a quiver.' She produced a cigarette, and put it in her mouth. Flick, flick, flick went her lighter. 'Talk about rest in peace. This place is *comatose*. No spirits that I can sense.' Delora can speak quite clearly even when she has a smoking cigarette hanging out of her mouth. I don't know how she does it.

'But the broken dishes!' Samantha protested. 'The little trail of throat lozenges!'

'Sweetie, I'm only telling you what I *felt*. I felt nothing. Which isn't to say that I'm not having an off day. It happens.' Delora coughed a hacking cough, giving Richard time to interrupt.

'I'll have a go tonight,' he said. 'Just to see. Everyone else can slope off to the pub, and leave me with my cameras for a couple of hours.'

'Yes, that's a good idea.' Delora nodded. 'I might even join you. Now, what else is going on? What's this about a ghost with no eyes?'

It surprises me the way Delora, who's supposed to be a psychic, always has to be told things – like people's names. You'd think she'd already know them, wouldn't you? But she doesn't. She's as keen to hear gossip as Mum is. So we went into the kitchen, drank tea, ate pumpkin scones and talked about Golden Gully. I didn't really *want* to talk about it, mind you, but I didn't have much choice. Everyone else was too interested. And I must admit that I didn't have to put up with a lot of snorts and titters and sidelong looks when the word 'ghost' was uttered. Richard and Delora are quite comfortable with the idea of ghosts. They don't think you're a weirdo just because you raise the possibility of a house (or a gully) being haunted. They're even willing to visit the gully, and take electromagnetic readings, and try to break through to the spirit realm.

'But not now,' Richard said. 'Not with everything happening over there. Maybe tomorrow morning, on our way home. When those poor boys have been . . . um . . . sorted out.'

'Yes, I hope they're going to be all right,' said Samantha. 'I wonder if we can do anything to help? What do you think, Hessel?'

Hessel grunted, and shook his head.

104

'No, you're right,' his wife agreed. 'We'd probably only get in the way. Tell you what, though – why don't we have dinner at the pub tonight? With Judy? The poor thing, she'll need a stiff drink after what she's been through today. What do you think, Hessel?'

'Yeah, all right,' Hessel growled.

'Did you hear that, Allie?' Samantha turned to me. 'Tell your mother we'll stop by on our way to the pub, and pick her up. You too, if you want. Tell her we'll make it about . . . let's see . . . seven-thirty? We'll pick her up then.'

'If we're still there,' I murmured. Glancing at my watch, I saw that it was nearly four. Getting late, in other words. 'We'd better go now,' I said. 'Mum will be wondering where we are. Thanks for the scones. Bye, Richard. Bye, Delora.'

But Michelle and I weren't allowed to make such an easy escape. Delora wanted to check out some of the Hill End sights before everything closed, and insisted that she and Richard drop us at the camping area. Then, when we arrived, she made a point of talking to Mum, who had to fill her in on the latest developments. It seemed that an ambulance had taken Tony, Jesse and Mrs Karavias to Mudgee hospital. No one yet knew what Tony's condition might be, though Jesse seemed okay; he had only gone with Tony because it was felt that a doctor should look at him, just to be on the safe side. Mrs Patel had decided to accompany them both. She had been told that the police would probably have to interview Jesse once he'd been examined by a doctor, and she wanted to be on hand when *that* happened. Our bus was supposed to pick her up in Mudgee at two o'clock the next day.

Meanwhile, we kids were supposed to carry on with our scheduled activities, and be good for the parents who were now in charge of our welfare.

'Which I suppose means that we carry on with that gold-panning session tomorrow morning,' Mum remarked in a worried voice, as Tammy's mum and Amy's dad and Delora and Richard clustered around. 'I mean, we've booked it. We've paid for it. And I suppose it can't do any harm – as long as we don't let the kids wander off anywhere.'

'What gold-panning session?' asked Amy's dad. 'What are you talking about?'

'Oh, there's some guide who's going to show us how to pan for gold,' Mum replied. 'Isn't that right, Esme?'

Tammy's mum nodded. 'He will come here tomorrow,' she confirmed. 'Eight-thirty, Mrs Patel said. He will go with us, show us some things . . . how to find gold.'

'*Real* gold?' It was Amy, hovering behind her dad. 'You mean there's still gold out there?'

'I doubt it,' her father retorted. 'You'd have to be pretty damned lucky. This place has been picked clean.'

It was then, because of what Amy's dad said, that I suddenly had my idea.

My idea about Abel Harrow, and how he might be made to stop chasing people.

CHAPTER # eight

'No,' said Michelle.

The stars were out, and sausages were still crackling and spitting away on the barbecue. Michelle and I had eaten one each, with bread (but no butter), tomatoes, lettuce, fried onion, and a couple of shortbread biscuits. Our greasy plates were sitting on the grass, beside our half-empty cans of soft drink. Mum wasn't with us; she had gone to the pub with Samantha, Delora and Hessel. Peter wasn't with us either; he had got up and joined the line near the barbecue, where he was waiting for another sausage. So I had decided to explain my idea to Michelle – quickly, before Peter returned – in the hope that she would think it a good one.

She didn't, at first.

'But this bracelet is Mum's!' she protested, covering it with her hand. 'She lent it to me!'

'Yes, I realise that.' Patiently, I tried to make her understand. 'I've been thinking about what you said, though. You said she only lent it to you because she never wore it. And you also said that we should do something about Abel Harrow. Well – this is something we could do.'

'I said we should *stop* him! I don't see how giving him my bracelet is going to stop him!'

'I thought you said it was your mum's bracelet?'

'What*ever*.' Michelle sounded really cross. 'It still doesn't make sense.'

'Michelle, I just *told* you. There are two good reasons why Abel might be hanging around Golden Gully. One is what you said before: that he's guarding a secret hoard of gold. That makes sense. Maybe he found it just before he died, and now he doesn't want anyone else going near it – even though it's not going to do *him* any good.' I took a deep breath, and glanced over at the sausage queue. In the faint light of various torches and lanterns, I could see that Peter was now at the head of it. 'Another good reason is that he might never have found any gold,' I continued. 'Maybe he spent his whole life searching for it, obsessing about it, and now he can't rest in peace until he finds some. So he's guarding his claim in case somebody else stumbles on a bit of gold there, and snatches it out from under his nose.'

'I still don't see why you want to bury my bracelet.'

'Because it might do the trick, Michelle. Once Eglantine finished her book, she could rest in peace. Maybe it's the same for Abel. Maybe, once he finds some gold – like your bracelet, for instance – he'll disappear. Because his hunger will be satisfied.'

Michelle gave a snort. 'Do you know how *busted* I'll be, if I bury Mum's bracelet?' she said.

'You can say you lost it. We're on a camping trip. People lose things on camping trips.'

'I'll still be busted!'

'I don't see why. If your mum doesn't wear it any more, why should she care what happens to it?'

A dark shape was heading in our direction: Peter, with his sausage. Leaning forward, I addressed Michelle in an urgent whisper.

'Just think about it,' I urged. 'I've still got to work out how we're going to get back to Golden Gully, tomorrow. Or maybe Richard can do the job for us. He said he's going to stop there in the morning, and check it out.'

'Check what out?' asked Peter. He sat down next to me, his sausage rolling around on his paper plate.

'Nothing,' I replied.

'Are you still talking about Tony and Jesse?'

'No.' We had already discussed Jesse's police interview (when it would happen, where it would happen, how it would be conducted) until we were blue in the face. 'I can't believe you're having another one of those things.'

'They're awful, aren't they?' Peter agreed, with a beaming smile. 'They look like great big turds and they taste like great big turds. I suppose it makes sense, though. Aren't sausage skins made of pig-guts, or something? Guts are where turds come from, after all.'

'Oh, please,' Michelle objected, screwing up her face. 'Don't be disgusting.'

'Amy's dad can't cook for nuts, can he?' I said, in an attempt to change the subject. 'I wonder why he volunteered?'

'He didn't.' Peter began to saw away at his charred sausage. 'Angus's dad did it last night, so it was someone else's turn tonight. Angus's dad cooks a *great* sausage,' he added, and flourished a battered morsel on the end of his fork. 'Sure you don't want one?'

'No, thanks.'

'*Sure?*'

He stuck the thing in my face, grinning fiendishly. When I pushed it away, I managed to up-end his plate, causing bits of burnt sausage to spill over the grass.

'Oh,' I said, feeling guilty. 'Sorry.'

'It's okay,' he sighed.

'You shouldn't wave those things at me.' I couldn't understand what he had been trying to do. It wasn't *like* Peter to act so . . . well, so Bethan-ish. 'It's scary.'

'I know. They're dangerous.' He stood up. 'Well –
back to the line, again.'

'It's quite short, now,' I offered, raising my voice, as
he headed for the barbecue. Then I turned to
Michelle.

'Where was I? Oh, yes. The bracelet,' I murmured,
and she shook her head.

'It's too much of a waste,' she replied.

'Even if it gets rid of Abel Harrow?'

'We won't know that, though, will we? We'll never
know. We'll walk away and never know.'

'Not necessarily. Not if Richard's with us. He might
be able to get some readings.'

'Richard with the glasses, you mean?' Michelle
seemed sceptical. 'I don't know, Allie. He didn't seem
to believe in Abel. And he didn't look very . . . I
mean, he looked a bit . . .' She searched for the right
words, but I could sense what she was trying to say.
Richard wasn't old enough. He wasn't serious enough.
He didn't have white hair and a dark suit and a foreign
accent.

'Richard is good,' I assured her. 'He knows what he's
doing. And he's got lots of equipment.'

Michelle made a face. I decided that Richard must
have really offended her when he questioned the fact
that Abel was a ghost.

'Honestly.' I didn't know how to convince her. 'He
was the one who filmed Eglantine's writing, remember? Appearing on the wall. You haven't seen him in

action.' And all at once, something occurred to me. 'Do you *want* to see him in action? Because you could.'

'Huh?'

'We could go up to Samantha's house and watch him. Right now. If you want to.'

It took Michelle a moment to work out what I meant.

'Oh!' she said. 'You mean that stuff he's doing up there? To see if he can spot Eustace?'

'That's happening right now.'

She glanced towards the road, which was lost in shadow. I watched her push her gold bracelet up and down her wrist.

There was a long silence.

'We'll need a torch,' she said at last.

'We've got one. It's in the tent.'

'They'll never let us.'

'Who? Amy's dad?' I peered at him; he was standing at the barbecue, waving smoke out of his eyes. His face glimmered with sweat in the light of a kerosene lantern. 'He won't mind. We'll tell him we're visiting Samantha.'

'But she's not there.'

'Yeah, but *he* doesn't know that, does he? He probably thinks that Mum's up at the house having dinner. And it's only a ten-minute walk.'

Michelle tucked a strand of hair behind one ear. She giggled.

'D'you think we could?' she asked.

'Do you want to?'

By now she was grinning. 'Yeah,' she said. 'Do you?'

'If it'll get you to bury your bracelet.' I found myself smiling back at her. 'Why are you laughing?'

'I'm not laughing.'

'Yes, you are.' We were both giggling like idiots all of a sudden. 'Stop it, will you?'

'It's like an adventure story,' Michelle spluttered. 'Creeping through the night to a haunted house . . .'

'I'll get the torch. You go and tell Amy's dad.'

The torch was on the floor of our tent, lost beneath a whole heap of sleeping-bag covers and dirty laundry and damp towels. It took me a while to find the thing – especially since I had to grope around in the dark. When I finally emerged, Michelle was back. And she had brought Peter with her.

'He wants to know if he can come,' she explained, shooting me an apologetic look. I was very put out. If Peter comes with us, I thought, he'll spread it around afterwards and it will be like Eglantine all over again. Ghost noises in the school playground. People springing out of cupboards with sheets draped over them. Jesse Gerangelos calling me a loony-tune.

'You haven't got your sausage,' I pointed out, fixing my eyes on his empty paper plate.

'I can do without,' he assured me. 'Really. It would be a *pleasure*.'

'We're just going up to Samantha's house.'

'The shack. I know. I'd like to see it – if that's okay.

114

Sounds interesting.' Peter glanced from me to Michelle, and back again. 'What's up? What's the matter? Is there a problem?'

I hesitated.

'Do I smell, or something?' he went on. 'Hey – I can take it. Boy germs. That's it. You're scared of boy germs.'

'Don't be stupid,' I said crossly, because I felt bad. I hate all that 'You're-not-our-friend-so-you-can't-play-with-us' sort of stuff. I've had to put up with it too many times myself, in the playground. And Peter was a nice guy. I didn't want to upset him.

'Look,' I began, and paused. Michelle and I exchanged glances.

'Are you two up to something?' Peter inquired. 'What happens up at that shack – do you smoke mari-juana, or run around in the nude?'

'Of course not!' I snapped, wondering if he could be persuaded to keep his mouth shut. Michelle raised an eyebrow at me. I tugged at my bottom lip. Peter gave a great sigh.

'Are you going to tell me, or not?' he said. 'Because if it's a secret, I can keep a secret, you know.'

'Really?' I peered at him. 'Cross your heart?'

'Cross my heart. Um . . . as long as you're not going to blow something up.'

He was joking, so I ignored him. Instead I asked, abruptly, if he remembered Eglantine – and he fixed me with a very intent look.

115

'Yea-ah,' he replied. 'Sort of. You never talked about her at school, much.'

'No. Because people always think you're weird, when you believe in ghosts.'

'I don't think you're weird,' he said promptly. 'Not *very* weird.'

'So you believe in them?'

'Well . . .' He thought for a moment. 'I don't *not* believe in them.'

'Allie,' Michelle interrupted. She was jiggling about as if she needed to go to the toilet. 'If we don't get up there soon, we might be too late.'

'Don't worry.' I knew that Richard could sit up all night, and not necessarily spot a thing. But it *was* eight-thirty, and we had to be in bed by ten. 'Look,' I said to Peter, 'you can come if you want to, but don't tell anybody, okay?'

'Okay. But –'

'Do you have a torch in your tent?'

'Yes, but –'

'Could you get it, please? Quickly.'

'Okay, but –'

'I told Amy's dad we'd only be an hour,' Michelle remarked. 'Still – I don't suppose he'll notice if we're a *little* longer. I think,' she added, 'that he's a bit pissed off with your mum, Allie. He's cross that she went off to dinner with her friends.'

It didn't take Peter long to fetch his torch. Even so, by the time he'd caught up with Michelle and me, we were already picking our way up the road to Samantha's. It was easier than I'd thought it would be, because the moon was practically full, and there was hardly a cloud in the sky. Even without our torches, we would have been able to see where we were going. Crickets cheeped. The air was very still. Glossy leaves and tin roofs gleamed in the moonlight.

Rustles in the long grass were probably lizards, unless they were little marsupials.

'So what's this big secret?' Peter inquired, after he had got his breath back.

'Shh!' I hissed. 'Not so loud!'

'Why? Are we sneaking in?' Michelle whispered. 'Isn't Richard supposed to know we've arrived?'

'We shouldn't disturb him,' I answered quietly. 'It might ruin everything. We'll just take a peek through a window. Once you've seen all his equipment set up, we'll leave.'

'What equipment?' Peter sounded bewildered, even though his voice was pitched low. 'Who's Richard? Why are you doing this?'

'Richard is a friend of ours,' I explained. 'There's supposed to be a ghost in Samantha's house, so Richard's trying to see if he can record any evidence that it's really there.' I stumbled on a pothole, and dropped my torch. 'Ouch!'

'You're *kidding* me!' Peter squeaked, clapping his hand over his mouth as Michelle glared at him. 'But that's fantastic!' he went on, much more softly. 'You mean he's a ghost-buster?'

'No,' I growled. 'There's no such thing.'

'Shh!' Michelle flapped a hand at us. 'Keep it down! We're nearly there!'

I recognised the fence when we reached it because it was overgrown with prickly rose bushes and honey-suckle. The rusty old gate looked as if it would squeal like a pig if touched, and I tried to remember if the hinges squeaked. I asked Michelle about this, in a whisper, but she couldn't recall.

Suddenly she clutched my wrist.

'Look!' she breathed. 'Over there!'

She pointed, not at the house, but at a stretch of garden near it. The house itself was dark, its ver-andahs wrapped in shadow; only its roof and chimney were clearly visible in the moonlight. Here and there, clumps of black trees also seemed to swallow up the moon's radiance. Between them, however, lay stretches of milky grass – looking almost like ice – and one of these stretches was being crossed by someone wearing trousers.

A man, I thought, instinctively ducking. Michelle did the same. 'Is that Richard?' Peter hissed, and we both flapped our hands frantically to shut him up.

The silhouette was sneaking towards the house. Peering over the top of a cascade of honeysuckle, I saw a hunched shadow disappear behind the dunny, then re-emerge briefly before it was screened by a may bush that grew near the back verandah. I heard a board creak. I heard a faint jingling sound.

'Was that Richard?' Michelle muttered. 'It looked too fat.'

'It was.' I gave the gate an experimental push, and winced as the hinges groaned. Michelle put her hands over her ears. Peter leaned towards me.

'Who was that?' he sighed.

I shrugged, biting my thumb.

'It wasn't a *burglar*, was it?' Michelle sounded scared. 'Allie?'

'I don't know! Shh!'

'Should we call the police?'

'I don't *know*, Michelle!' Then it occurred to me. 'Richard's inside. He might have a mobile.'

At that very instant, we all heard a noise – a faraway crashing noise, like someone dropping a handful of saucepan lids. There followed a muffled shout. Michelle and I stared at each other, but Peter was already shoving his way through the gate, which shrieked mournfully on its hinges.

'Look!' he rasped. 'See? There's a light on, now!' Bent almost double, he gestured with the beam of his torch, and I spotted a golden glow coming from somewhere beyond the depths of the front verandah.

'Peter!' I croaked. 'Wait! Don't go in there!'

'I'm not,' he assured me. 'I just want to see if I can –'

'*Peter!*' Michelle squeaked. 'Get *down!*'

'Shh!' I'd heard something. 'Listen!'

119

Voices – I could hear voices. They were male voices, and not very clear, but they weren't shouting. A low rumble was followed by a pause, and another low rumble.

They were coming from somewhere behind the house.

'Do you hear that?' said Peter. 'They're talking.'

'Maybe we'd better go back,' I replied doubtfully. 'Maybe this wasn't a good idea.'

'But can't we just take a look?' he pleaded. 'Isn't that all you were going to do anyway? Just peek through the window?'

'I guess . . .'

'What about Richard?' Michelle reminded me. 'Hadn't we better make sure he's safe?'

She was right, I realised. We couldn't just sneak away. So we crept around the back of the house, dimming our torches with the palms of our hands, until we reached the may bush. From behind its drooping fronds, we could see the kitchen window (which was all lit up) and the kitchen door, which was standing open. We could also hear the voices, quite clearly.

'. . . you want to borrow some coffee, you shouldn't do it while your neighbours are out,' Richard was saying, in his rapid-fire way. 'If that's what you *were* doing, which I seriously doubt, by the way.'

In reply, somebody mumbled something about not being a thief.

'Then what were you doing with Samantha's coffee?' Richard demanded.

'I was running low, I told ya –'

'So you decided to stick a little pile of coffee beans in the cutlery drawer?'

'. . . accident . . .'

'Come on, Mr Bourne. Give me some credit.'

Richard didn't sound frightened at all. He *certainly* didn't sound as if he was talking to a ghost. Craning my neck, I caught a glimpse of the top of his head through the kitchen window, and realised that he was carrying a torch, like me.

For a moment I wondered why he didn't just turn on the light – before remembering that Samantha and Hessel didn't have any lights to turn on.

'You've been coming in here, haven't you, Mr Bourne?' Richard continued. 'Coming in and re-arranging things. Things like those coffee beans.' Another pause. 'Oh, come on. You let yourself in. You've got a key. Why do you have a key? How did you get it?'

A mumble.

'What's that?'

'I said *Evie gave it to me!*'

Michelle sucked in her breath. We exchanged glances.

'Evie?' said Richard. 'Who's Evie?'

'She used ta live here!' an angry voice retorted. 'This used ta be her kitchen, until those two fancy-pants

121

tore the bloody guts out of it! She must be turning in her grave, to see what they've done! Ripped up all her daffs and her pansies to stick that bloody oven in, down the back! Letting all her roses go to buggery! You're right, I've been messing with stuff in here because I thought I might get rid of the two of 'em, the dozey bloody hippies, but they're too thick to know what's good for 'em!'

'Ah,' said Richard, and I had to see. I just had to see who was talking to him. But when I carefully skirted the may bush, and put my foot on the bottom step, it creaked horribly.

The conversation stopped. Michelle tugged at my jumper.

'Who's there?' said Richard.

I took my foot off the bottom step – but it creaked again. Peter and Michelle were hissing things that I couldn't understand. Then the beam of Richard's torch hit my face.

He had emerged through the kitchen door.

'*Allie?*' he exclaimed.

'Oh – uh – hi.'

'What are you *doing* here?'

'We were just – um –'

'*We*? Who's *we*?'

I glanced at Michelle, who was sort of shrinking back into the darkness, as if she wanted to make a run for it. Unfortunately, that was no longer possible.

I pulled an apologetic face.

'Just my friends,' I explained. 'You've met Michelle. And this is Peter.'

Peter stepped into the light, clicking his torch off. He said: 'We wanted to see a ghost. Uh . . . Allie said you were looking for one.'

'That's right,' Richard replied. He gazed at the three of us for a few seconds, thoughtfully. 'I *was* looking for a ghost. And I seem to have found him. Kids . . .' He swung the beam of his own torch around until it was fixed on his companion. 'Meet Mr Alf Bourne.'

CHAPTER # nine

Alf Bourne was very old. His face drooped, his hair was white, and there were big, brown spots all over his hands. He wore dark blue trousers and a flannelette shirt, and he was sitting on one of Samantha's rickety bentwood chairs, which looked as if it might collapse any minute.

He stared at us with watery, red-rimmed eyes, nursing a small plastic torch in his lap.

'Mr Bourne is Samantha's next-door neighbour,' Richard went on, as Peter and Michelle and I trooped into the kitchen. 'He must have thought there was nobody home, because I hadn't lit the lamps.'

Mr Bourne muttered something about damn fools sitting around in the dark, and other people never going anywhere without making a noise. Richard closed the kitchen door.

'Apparently Mr Bourne doesn't like Samantha or Hessel,' he said, 'so he's been sneaking in here and rearranging their things. Pretending to be a ghost.'

'Only a bloody fool doesn't change the locks when they move into a new house,' was Mr Bourne's response.

'So Eustace doesn't exist?' Michelle asked, turning to Richard, and he shrugged.

'Eustace the ghost certainly doesn't,' he replied. 'For all I know, Eustace the child didn't either.'

'Of course he did!' Mr Bourne flushed, and sat up straight. 'He was Evie's boy, poor little beggar. Died of pneumonia, back in '48, and I thought she'd never get over it. That's why . . .' He trailed off, suddenly, his flush fading.

'That's why what?' Richard prompted, more gently, and Mr Bourne made a sweeping gesture with his hand, as if to say 'what the hell'.

'About a week after the poor kid died, Evie found a pile of buttons and things behind a dresser – things that Eustace must have left there before he passed,' Mr Bourne confessed. 'She got the idea in her head that his spirit was still around the place, and she was happy about it.'

A long pause. At last Richard said: 'So you kept sneaking in and leaving little piles of things around the house. To keep her happy.'

'Yeah,' Mr Bourne admitted, with a sigh. Michelle and I looked at each other. We couldn't believe it, especially since everything around us seemed almost dream-like: the pale old man, the torch-light, the creepy kitchen. I tried to imagine sneaking into the house of *our* next-door neighbour, pretending to be a ghost, but I couldn't.

Richard took off his glasses, and polished them on the hem of his shirt. The silence stretched out. I wondered what he was going to do.

Surely he wouldn't call the police? Mr Bourne looked so *old*.

'Well,' Richard sighed, pushing his glasses back on, 'I'm very sorry for your loss, Mr Bourne, but – well, you have been trespassing, you know.'

Mr Bourne gazed at him sullenly, hands trembling.

'I mean, I do sympathise,' Richard continued, 'but it's really not on. You know that, don't you? It's not nice.'

Mr Bourne scratched the back of his neck, avoiding Richard's reproachful gaze. Richard said, 'So am I to understand that you actually have a key, Mr Bourne? A key to this house?'

He did. He fumbled around in his pocket and pulled out a brass key. 'No point now, anyway,' he mumbled, dropping the key into Richard's outstretched hand. 'You've spoiled the fun, now.'

'Samantha and Hessel wouldn't call it fun, Mr Bourne.'

'No?' The old man's watery eyes glinted. 'Well, they're a funny pair, aren't they? Not normal.'

'I don't think Evie would have approved, do you?'

But that was the wrong thing to say. Mr Bourne glared at Richard fiercely. 'What do you know about Evie?' he snapped, and shuffled to the door, muttering under his breath. He was still muttering as he made his way down the back steps.

'Are you all right, Mr Bourne?' Richard called after him. 'Can you manage?'

No reply. We watched Mr Bourne trudge towards the fence that separated his house from Samantha's, a beam of light flickering over the ground ahead of him. I said to Richard (very quietly): 'Do you think he's a bit . . . you know . . . funny in the head?'

'Perhaps.' Richard pushed his spectacles up his nose, and sighed. 'But that doesn't mean he isn't grieving. He must have loved Evie Harrow very much, don't you think? He probably would have hated anyone who moved into Evie's house. He would have tried to scare them away no matter who they were, or what they did.'

'With little piles of buttons and paperclips?' asked Michelle sceptically.

'And broken dishes,' I added. 'And a possible ghost. You know what a lot of people are like, when they have to deal with ghosts.'

'Speaking of ghosts, I don't think *you* lot have any reason to hang around,' said Richard, whose voice changed all of a sudden. He put one hand on his hip. With the other, he shone his torch right in my face again. 'Since this one was a hoax, you can get back to where you should be. What on earth do you think you're playing at, sneaking around in the dark?'

I felt embarrassed, because I hate it when clever people like Richard catch me doing silly things. 'Michelle just wanted to see your stuff,' I mumbled.

'What stuff?'

'You know. Your PRISM stuff.'

'Why?'

I didn't want to tell him, not with Peter listening. To my horror, it was Michelle who answered the question, in a roundabout sort of way.

'Are you going to Golden Gully, tomorrow morning? Allie thought you might be,' she said.

Richard's torch-beam shifted, coming to rest on Michelle's upturned face.

'Golden Gully,' he murmured, adjusting his glasses again. 'Well . . . I mean . . . it did cross my mind.' His voice became grave, too grave, almost as if he was making fun of Michelle. 'Since you and Allie seem so convinced that there's an eyeless ghost out there, chasing people into holes.'

Aaagh. I couldn't bring myself to look at Peter. I could only imagine the expression on his face.

'So you're going first thing?' Michelle pressed, apparently unaware that she was making a fool of herself in front of witnesses. I fluttered my hands at her.

'Don't worry about it, Michelle,' I said, trying to quell her with an accusing stare.

'What do you mean?' She frowned. 'I thought you wanted to bury the bracelet?'

'And I thought you didn't.'

'I've changed my mind.'

'You've changed your *mind*?'

'You convinced me.' A smile tweaked at the corner of her mouth; she leaned towards me, cupping her hand around my ear, and buzzed: 'Chasing ghosts is a lot of fun, isn't it?'

'Yeah – well – let's talk about it later on.' I jerked my head at Peter, who said calmly: 'Don't mind me. I won't say a word.'

'Sorry – is there a problem?' Richard asked. 'Is there something you want me to do?'

'No,' I said.

'Yes,' said Michelle. 'You see, Allie thinks that, if Abel Harrow *is* a ghost, he might be hanging around Golden Gully because he can't bear to leave until he finds some gold. She thinks he mightn't ever have found any gold when he was alive, you see, and he's so obsessed that he's haunting the place. So if we put some gold there for him to find, he might disappear. The way Eglantine did when her book was finished.'

I rubbed my hand across my eyes, wishing that the whole idea didn't sound so stupid when announced in a loud voice to a grown man. Shooting a glance at

Peter, I saw that his gaze was fixed on me, and I couldn't help blushing.

'I know it sounds stupid,' I blurted out. 'It was just an idea.'

Richard scratched his head. For once, his voice was slow and hesitant.

'Well . . . it's not a *bad* idea,' he finally remarked. 'I suppose it does make sense . . . if he is a ghost . . . it's as good an idea as any . . .'

Meaning he thought it sounded stupid. *I'm* not stupid. I could tell that he wasn't convinced.

'Anyway, we thought we'd use my bracelet, because it's made of gold,' Michelle finished. 'We thought we'd bury it in Golden Gully, where Abel's bound to find it. Or maybe you could bury it for us, since you're going back there. We don't know if we will be.'

'Your bracelet? Oh, no.' Richard's tone was getting more and more reluctant. 'You don't want to do that. A gold bracelet? That's worth money.'

'It's only nine carat,' Michelle pointed out.

'It's still worth money.'

'Yes, but the chain isn't gold. Only the charms. It didn't cost much.'

'I don't think so, Michelle. Really I don't.'

'But it might work! Don't you think?'

'Yes, it might, I suppose.' Richard didn't want to hurt my feelings; I could tell. 'But even so . . . I mean, it's throwing good money away . . .'

'I don't care,' Michelle said mulishly.

'I bet your mum would care.'

'No, she wouldn't. She never wears this bracelet. She gave it to me.'

'Then that's another reason why you shouldn't throw it away.'

'I'll just tell her I lost it.'

'Oh, no.' Richard was looking more and more flustered. 'You mustn't lie to your mother.'

'Why not?' Michelle snapped. 'She lies to me! She said she made me come here for my own good, when all she wants to do is go away with her new boyfriend! Well, if she wants me to go camping, then she'll just have to put up with me losing jewellery, won't she? People *always* lose things on camping trips!'

Poor Michelle. I don't think she meant to say all that; normally she's so cool about her mum's boyfriends. I caught Peter's eye, and then we turned away from each other to study the floor at our feet. Richard was demolished – he's a very sensitive sort of guy. He even began to stutter. 'But – but – but –' he said.

'It's none of your business what I do with my things,' Michelle squeaked, in a halting, furious tone that I've only heard coming out of her mouth once or twice. (She rarely loses her temper.) Richard threw up his hands.

'Okay! Okay!' he cried. 'I'll do it! I'll go there and I'll leave it in the – where do you want me to leave it, anyway? Where did you see him? Anywhere in particular?'

I gazed at Michelle. She gazed at me. It was hard to put into words.

'Just anywhere?' Richard said. 'Or near that mine-shaft, maybe? Where the boys fell in? Where is that? It would be a good place to start scanning for traces.'

I put a finger in my mouth. Michelle seemed to sag, like a balloon with its air escaping. 'It would be better if we could show you,' she faltered.

'You can't tell me?' Richard seemed tired all of a sudden, and perhaps a little cross. 'Have you got a map or anything?'

'You don't need a map,' Peter said quietly. 'Tambaroora Creek runs through Golden Gully, and the fossicking area is just north of that. If you all go early – at eight o'clock, say – then you can meet up with everyone else down the creek at nine. It would be easy.'

I couldn't believe my ears. He sounded so calm and sensible and sort of – I don't know, sort of *grown up*. As we all stared at him, he added: 'The whole group is going fossicking down at Tambaroora Creek tomorrow. Then we're having lunch, and then we're leaving. That's why, if you guys visit the gully before eight-thirty, it should work out pretty well.'

This sounded like a sensible suggestion to me.

Richard put his head on one side, considering it. I asked him if he *could* pick us up tomorrow. At eight o'clock, say?

'Well, gee, I don't know – I mean, I suppose so – if your mother lets you – I mean, if *your* mother lets you, Allie, not yours – oh, all right. Yes, all right, we'll make it an early start. If your mum says it's okay.'

I don't think I was wrong in believing that we had hassled the poor guy into doing something he didn't want to do. Peter clearly felt the same way. 'Gosh,' he said, after Richard had quickly shown us his tape-recorder, his time-lapse camera, and his infra-red equipment, and had told us to wait by the car, 'you really twisted his arm, Michelle.'

'I did not!' she snapped. 'Don't be mean.'

'I'm not being mean. I think it was cool.'

'Don't,' I said. Michelle seemed to be in a funny mood and I didn't want her teased. I also wondered if I'd been a bit ungrateful – I mean about her bracelet and everything. It had been my idea, after all. 'Thanks, Michelle,' I murmured. 'It's really nice of you to give up your bracelet.'

'I know.'

'Do you think you should melt it down?' Peter suggested. 'So it would look more like the kind of gold you'd find in Golden Gully?' As we both stared at him, he shrugged and spread his hands. 'Just a thought,' he said. 'Don't mind me.'

At that point Richard joined us; he'd been locking up the house. He insisted on driving us back to the camping ground and also instructed us, when we reached our destination, not to go wandering off at night.

'It's dangerous,' he said firmly.

'But we didn't go far,' I pointed out, slamming the front passenger door. 'We just wanted to –'

'Yes, yes, I know, you told me. You still shouldn't be wandering around at night. Any more of it and I'll tell your mum.'

'Okay.' There was no point arguing. 'See you tomorrow.'

'What? Oh – right.'

'You will come?'

'Yes, of course, don't worry.'

'Bye then.'

'Bye, Mr Boyer.'

'Are you disappointed, Mr Boyer?' Peter asked, out of the blue, and Richard peered at him through the car window.

'About what?' Richard queried.

'About Eustace. Not being real.'

'Oh . . .' Richard shrugged. 'They hardly ever are. They're always either a hoax or something structural – dicky plumbing or rats in the ceiling or woodwork contracting in the heat. Something like that.' He waved us away from the car. 'Goodnight,' he finished, and drove off towards the hotel.

'I guess he must be going to tell Mum what happened,' I observed, watching his red tail-lights recede. 'I hope she's not too cross.'

'Do you think your mum'll let us? Go back to the gully, I mean,' Michelle inquired.

'Who knows?'

'We ought to.'

'Yeah.'

'Just in case Richard gets the wrong place. If he gets the wrong place, Abel might never find the bracelet.'

I had to agree, though in my heart of hearts I didn't really want to return to Golden Gully. The place had me spooked. In fact I couldn't understand why Michelle was so keen. Perhaps she was more of an adventure-story type than I'd realised. Or perhaps it was because she had never actually seen Abel Harrow, or heard Jesse screaming from the bottom of the mine shaft.

She hadn't felt that nasty sensation in her guts.

'We'll ask Mum when she gets back,' I sighed. 'Maybe if we go with Richard and Delora, she won't mind so much.'

Michelle nodded. She pushed her bracelet up her arm, and announced that she had to go to the toilet. Behind us the camping ground was fairly peaceful; Amy's dad was cleaning the barbecue hotplate and Angus's dad was organising the washing-up. Nobody was fooling around, I noticed. Without Jesse and

Tony there to get Malcolm going, even he seemed to be behaving himself.

Michelle strolled off to the toilet block ('Wish me luck,' she sighed, because she hates public toilets) and Peter pulled a packet of jelly beans out of his pocket.

'Want one?' he asked.

'No, thanks.' I took a deep breath. 'You probably think we're crazy, with all this ghost stuff.'

'Not me,' he said politely.

'Like I said before, people always think you're weird, when you believe in ghosts.'

'Not me,' he repeated.

'Other people do, though. People like Malcolm Morling.' I lowered my voice a little. 'Do you think you could maybe . . . you know . . . keep it to yourself? About Abel, and everything? And Eustace, of course.'

'Sure.' Peter put the jelly beans back in his pocket, scratched his arm, rubbed his nose, and pulled his cap down low over his eyes. All at once I had an idea. I don't know where it came from. Maybe I felt that a bribe might keep him from shooting his mouth off. Maybe I felt as if he deserved a reward. Or maybe I just knew, deep down, that he was dying to be included and I couldn't bring myself to disappoint him.

'You can come with us tomorrow morning,' I said gruffly. 'If Mum lets us go.'

He grinned at me. 'Yeah?'

'That's if you want to.'

'Sure! I want to. That would be *great.*'

I couldn't understand why he thought so. But then again, I didn't know him very well at the time.

Personally, I wasn't looking forward to the trip at all.

CHAPTER # ten

I was very clever about asking Mum if we could go to Golden Gully. I waited until she came home (at ten o'clock), saw that she was feeling happy and relaxed after a good meal, a bottle of wine and a few laughs with some old friends, and pestered her until she would have said anything to get me off her back. Then, when she woke up the next morning, she couldn't withdraw her permission – even though she was beginning to have doubts.

'But I can't come with you, Allie,' she objected. 'I've missed two dinners, so the least I can do is supervise the breakfast and the packing up. I'll be stuck here all morning.'

'It doesn't matter. Richard and Delora will be with us.'

'But you'll miss the fossicking.'

'No, we won't. It won't take an hour. We'll meet you down at the fossicking area. Richard will drive us.'

'But you don't know where the fossicking area is.'

'Yes, we do. Peter does. He's got a map.'

'But you've already been to Golden Gully. Why do you want to go back?'

I told her the truth – at least, most of the truth. I told her that Abel might be a ghost, and that Richard needed to know where he should scan for electromagnetic readings. I didn't tell her about the bracelet. I knew that she wouldn't approve.

'But why do you all need to go?' she complained.

'Because I know where Abel hangs out, Peter knows where the fossicking area is, and Michelle doesn't want to be left behind with Malcolm Morling and Amy Driscoll.'

At last I got my way. I generally do when Mum has a lot on her mind – and she did, that morning. Everyone was packing up, Mrs Patel wasn't there to help organise things, and the bus-driver was requesting his instructions. Besides, I'm a good debater. Most people seem to give up when I argue with them.

'But I want you to be careful, Allie,' Mum stressed. 'No wandering off. Do you hear me? I mean it, Allie, if you wander away from Richard there'll be no TV for the rest of the year.'

'Okay, Mum.'

'You promise?'

'I promise.'

'The police will probably be around there anyway, looking for the old man,' she said. 'Police or National Parks people.'

But they weren't. When Richard pulled into the little Golden Gully parking area, just off Tambaroora Road, we saw at once that it was empty of other vehicles.

'Which isn't surprising, at this hour,' Richard remarked. I don't think he was too pleased about having to get up so early. He looked a bit puffy around the eyes, and he hadn't shaved.

Delora, on the other hand, was wide-awake and cheery, and wearing colours so bright that you practically needed sunglasses to look at her. She'd been talking ever since we got in the car, and she gave Richard a poke in the ribs whenever he started to mutter things about coffee or sleeping in.

'He's a coffee addict,' she confided, craning her neck to wink at the three of us who were crammed into the back seat. 'Can't function without his morning cuppa. I'm a ciggie addict and he's a coffee addict – that's why we get along so well.'

Michelle and I smiled politely. Then Richard parked the car, and we all climbed out. There was a chill in the air, and a fitful breeze chased small, fluffy clouds across the sky. I saw that Delora was wearing her high-heeled snakeskin boots; how, I wondered, did she expect to climb up gully walls in those things? Richard had brought his electromagnetic field detector, and Michelle had brought her bracelet. Peter was carrying his backpack, as usual.

Delora lit up a cigarette.

'Okay,' said Richard. 'Let's go, shall we?'

Everyone moved forward. Loose stones crunched under our feet. To my surprise, Delora had stopped talking; she swore occasionally, when she stumbled in those silly boots, but for the most part she was silent, puffing away on her cigarette and stopping, occasionally, to shut her eyes and take a deep, slow breath. I don't know what she was doing. Opening herself up to the spirits, perhaps? Or just recovering her strength?

By the time we reached the big arch she looked puffed out. (All those cigarettes, probably.)

'That's where I first saw the old man,' I volunteered, pointing. 'Down that little gully off to the side. That's where Jesse and Tony fell into the mineshaft, too – you go down there and walk a bit further, and then you go up over the edge of the gully wall.'

'We don't need to go that far,' said Richard. 'I suggest we start where you first saw the old man. Where was it?'

I showed him. Cautiously, with a hollow feeling in my stomach, I walked to the spot where I had first caught a glimpse of Abel Harrow. The light was falling differently now; the little gully was almost entirely wrapped in shadow. I shivered, and folded my arms across my chest.

'Here,' I murmured.

Richard stopped beside me. He waved his electro-magnetic field detector about, and checked the reading.

'Hmmm,' he grunted.

'Anything?' asked Michelle, from behind us.

Richard made a see-sawing motion with one hand. 'Could be,' he said. 'Let's keep going.'

We shuffled forward. The gully was so narrow, it made me uneasy. But we soon emerged into the sunlight again, as the narrow passage opened into a broad one.

'This is where I saw him the second time. Right here,' I announced, and felt someone tug at my sleeve. My heart skipped a beat, but it was only Michelle. She whispered: 'Is this where we should bury it, do you think?'

'I don't know.'

'Did you bring something to dig with? I didn't.'

'Neither did I.'

Suddenly a beat-up silver tablespoon was thrust under my nose. I turned, and saw that Peter was holding it. He lifted an eyebrow.

'Borrowed it from Tammy's mum,' he informed me, with a half-smile. 'We have to give it back, though.'

'Thanks, Peter.' I plucked it from his grip. 'You really think ahead.'

He couldn't help looking smug when I said that. It occurred to me that he was quite a smart and well-organised kind of guy, despite his weird jokes and sci-fi obsessions. Then suddenly Michelle said: 'What is it? Mr Boyer?', and I jerked my head around.

Richard had wandered down the gully a little way. He was standing very still, one finger pressed against his mouth, frowning at the gadget cradled in his hand. A puff of wind ruffled his curls.

As I watched, he raised his chin and began to peer around, very slowly and intently. I couldn't see his eyes too well, but from the way his head was thrust forward I was willing to bet that they were narrowed in concentration.

'What is it?' Michelle repeated, without getting an answer from Richard. It was Delora who spoke instead.

'I have to say that I don't like this,' she declared hoarsely. She had wrapped her arms around her fluffy, lime-green chest. Her smouldering cigarette stub was still tucked between the index and middle fingers of her right hand. Standing in the entrance to the smaller gully, teetering on her high heels, her shoulders hunched and her knees turned in, she looked very, very uncomfortable.

'Rickie?' she said, raising her rough-edged voice. 'Sweetie? We're not wanted here.'

'Mmm?' He turned his head slightly, his gaze still fixed on the electromagnetic field detector. 'What's that?'

'I said *we're not wanted here*. Let's go, eh?'

'Yes, hang on. In a minute.'

'What do you mean?' Michelle spoke before I could. She was staring at Delora with round, anxious eyes. 'What's wrong? Why are we not wanted?'

'I don't know, sweetie,' Delora replied. She dropped her cigarette butt onto the dirt and ground it out with the toe of her boot. I sensed, rather than saw, Peter wince beside me.

'This is an historical site,' he pointed out, stooping to retrieve the smouldering piece of litter. 'You shouldn't be throwing away cigarette butts.' But Delora didn't seem to hear him. She was glancing around nervously.

'Delora?' I said, in a loud voice. 'What's the matter, are you feeling something?'

'Only that we're not wanted.' She had started to jig up and down, as if she was cold. 'Rickie, we're not welcome. Sweetie? Let's not hang around.'

'Quick,' said Peter. He was shaking Michelle's arm. 'Come on. Let's bury it here.'

'What? Oh. Right.' Michelle removed her bracelet from her wrist. 'Who's going to dig the hole?'

'I will,' said Peter, then hesitated. 'Unless you want to?' he asked, offering me the spoon.

I shook my head.

'Hurry up,' Michelle urged. 'It's half past eight, already.'

Peter dropped down onto his haunches, and began to dig. He scraped away at the gravel, then at the finer dirt underneath it. Within seconds, he'd hollowed out a little pit, into which Michelle dropped her bracelet and Peter the cigarette butt. They both covered the pit with handfuls of dirt, which Peter started to pat down firmly.

From further down the gully, Richard remarked: 'This is interesting.'

'What?' said Delora.

'I was getting a reading of eight, and it just surged up into the region of eleven or twelve, and now it's back down to seven. What do you make of that?'

'I don't know,' Delora croaked. 'Something nasty. Come *on*.'

'Hey,' Peter exclaimed, 'this dirt feels . . .'

What happened next seemed to happen so quickly that I still don't know who screamed first. It might have been Michelle, as she lurched forward. It might have been Peter when he jumped up, as if he'd been burned. Or it might have been Delora, who grabbed my shoulder and nearly pulled it out of its socket.

'*Richard!*' she screeched.

'Who pushed me?' squealed Michelle. 'Someone pushed me!'

'Get out!' Delora yelled. 'Go on, go, go! *Richard! GO!*'

We went. We were in a total panic, stumbling and running and stumbling again. It was Delora who had frightened us. She kept nudging me from behind, urging us forward. Peter was panting: 'Something grabbed my hand – my hand got stuck!' Richard was pounding along behind us. 'Hey!' he called. 'Hey, wait! What is it? What?'

At last Delora slowed. She collapsed against the wall of the gully that lay under the big arch, wheezing and coughing and red in the face. Staggering up to her, Richard exclaimed, 'What's wrong? Del? What is it?'

'Oh, dear,' she hacked. 'Oh – oh, dear.'

'Are you all right?'

'Yes . . . yes . . .' More coughing.

'Who pushed me?' Michelle had stopped too. There were tears in her eyes. 'Did anyone here push me? Someone pushed me!'

'And something grabbed my hand,' Peter added, in a taut, shaken voice. 'I was patting down the dirt and my hand got stuck. Just for a second. I really had to *yank* it . . .'

'What on earth was that all about?' Richard wanted to know. 'Delora? Why did you scream?'

'Because . . . because . . .' She coughed, and took a deep breath, straightening up. 'Because we *weren't wanted*.'

'By whom?'

'I don't know.'

'Abel Harrow?'

'I don't know.' She shook her head, still gasping. 'God, those cigarettes. They're going to be the death of me. Oh! That was nasty.'

'What was?' Richard still sounded confused. 'Did you see something?'

'No, no. Didn't have to.' Cough, cough. 'Plain as day. Weren't wanted. Horrible energy.' Delora flapped her hands. 'Mustn't go back.'

'Did anyone else see anything?'

'Someone pushed me,' said Michelle, for at least the third time. 'I nearly fell over.'

'Are you sure you didn't just miss your footing?' Richard queried. 'I mean, when you heard Delora scream?' But Michelle stuck her bottom lip out.

'Someone pushed me,' she insisted.

'What about you, Allie? Did you see anything?'

I shook my head. There was a long silence. At last Peter said, in a small voice, 'Can you feel anything now, Delora?'

'No, no. We're fine here.'

'Then let's go,' Michelle squeaked. 'Come on.'

'Yes, you go to the car,' Richard agreed. 'I won't be a minute, I'll just duck back and check my readings – it probably wasn't anything, but I should run a test scan –'

'*NO!*' we all cried.

'But –'

'Sweetie,' said Delora, taking his arm, 'we've done what we came to do. You're not going back there.'

'But –'

'Rickie – angel – trust me. It won't do you any good.'

So we all returned to Richard's car. On the way, I found myself beside Peter, trailing behind the rest of them. (Michelle had taken the lead.) At first we didn't talk. After a while, though, he touched my elbow and said: 'Are you all right?'

I blinked at him.

'Yeah. Why?'

'You haven't said much.'

'Neither have you.'

'So you didn't . . . I mean . . .' He hesitated. 'Are you *sure* you didn't see anything?'

'Yes. I'm sure.' Why on earth would I lie? 'What about you?' I asked. 'Are you *sure* something grabbed your hand?'

'Yes.' He scratched his neck. 'Maybe.' A sigh. 'I don't know.'

'You don't know?'

'I'm not sure. Everything happened at once. Michelle nearly fell on me ...' He gave a helpless, hopeless little laugh. 'It was weird, though, wasn't it?'

'Very.'

He lowered his voice to a whisper. 'Is Delora for real?'

'I think so.' After a moment's thought, I added: 'Which isn't to say she can't be a bit odd, some-times.'

Peter fell silent. We walked on for a bit. I studied him out of the corner of my eye, noting how he was gnawing his lip and knitting his brows. At last I couldn't help myself. I really wanted to find out.

'Sorry you came?' I inquired, and his head jerked up.

'Hell, *no!*' he exclaimed. And he meant it.

Which was flattering, in a funny kind of way.

CHAPTER # eleven

We were all pretty shaken up. For a while, even Delora was silent. Richard wouldn't let her smoke in the car, so she sat flicking her lighter on, off, on, off until we reached the fossicking area, downstream from Golden Gully. Then she jumped out, lit up and began to inhale as if her life depended on it.

'Well,' said Richard, who remained sitting behind the wheel. 'That was very odd.' He peered around. 'Is this the right place?'

'It must be,' Peter replied. 'That's our bus.'

'Ah.'

'They must have gone down that path,' Peter added. 'We can ask Steve, I suppose.'

'Steve?'

'He's the bus driver.'

But we didn't have to ask Steve. Because when we got out of the car, and joined Delora, we could hear the distant sound of kids' voices. Somewhere down the path, through the bush, the remaining members of the Year Six excursion were being noisy, as usual.

'I'll just take them down,' Delora announced, as if we were babies. She was talking to Richard. 'Rickie? I'll just make sure they're all right.'

'You don't have to,' I objected.

'No, no, I will. Best to be on the safe side.' Delora shivered, suddenly, and sucked in a lungful of smoke. 'You shouldn't be wandering around this place by yourself.'

She was so obviously disturbed that it made us all uneasy. When I asked her if she and Richard would be visiting the museum, she stared at me as if I had a third nostril.

'The what?'

'The museum,' I repeated. 'You know. To check out the ghost of Granny Evans.' Slithering down a dusty slope in front of her, I had to grab at tree-trunks for support. 'Didn't Mum tell you? I thought she told you about Granny Evans.'

'Oh – uh – yeah. I think so.' She didn't sound too sure. 'We'll see. Maybe. Look – there's your mum. Hi, Jude! How are you, sweetie?'

I'll spare you all the details of our gold-panning session, which was supervised by a bloke called Mac. I suppose it was okay, though there was hardly any water in the creek to pan with, and Mac kept looking at his watch as if he had somewhere better to be. No one found any gold, of course – perhaps because no one's heart was really in it. We were all tired, wrung-out and (in the case of our bus driver) hung-over. By ten o'clock everyone had had enough, so we piled back into the bus and returned to the camp site, where we packed up our gear. Then we had lunch. When Mum asked me how our trip to Golden Gully had turned out, I replied that I wasn't sure. Something had happened, but I didn't know exactly what it was.

'You mean you saw something?' Mum inquired.

'No.'

'You got some readings?'

'I think so.'

'Are you all right, Allie?' She looked at me closely. 'What happened?'

'I don't know. Honestly. I really don't know.'

And I didn't want to explain myself further, because there were so many things to do and so many people around. Michelle and Peter and I didn't have a spare moment to discuss the Golden Gully business until we were back on the bus, where it turned out that we couldn't talk in case we were overheard. So we just sat there, eating our crisps and drinking our soft drinks, staring out the window, reflecting on our Golden Gully experience, until we stopped in Mudgee to pick up Mrs Patel.

Everyone was very surprised to see Jesse Gerangelos climb onto the bus behind her. I think we all got quite a shock when we spotted his slouching figure. I don't know what we'd expected, exactly – perhaps that he'd been whisked off into another world of police stations and hospital waiting rooms and school principal's offices, never to be seen again. In a funny sort of way he'd become almost unreal, as if he was part of an ancient legend. That's why it was a little odd to see him in the flesh.

He looked different, somehow. His hair was still black and wavy, and his eyelashes were still thick and glossy, and he still had those great teeth and those big eyes and all the other things that made him so good-looking. But the light had gone out of his face. He didn't look mischievous any more – just weary and distracted and glum.

He found himself an empty seat down the back, and threw himself into it without saying a word to anyone. Malcolm Morling settled in beside him. Amy asked: 'Are you okay, Jesse?'

A grunt was his only response. Up front, Mrs Patel began to converse with Mum as the bus pulled onto the road. The roar of the engine was so loud that I couldn't hear what they were saying.

'Did you talk to the cops?' Malcolm inquired, nudging Jesse in the ribs. He received a forceful shove in return.

'Piss off,' Jesse muttered, and Malcolm looked surprised.

'What's up with you?'

'Nothing.'

'Where's Tony?' Angus wanted to know.

'In hospital,' Jesse replied.

'Is he all right?'

'Why ask me?'

'Haven't you seen him?' said Peter, and Jesse turned on Peter like a cornered snake.

'No, I haven't!' he snapped – only he used a certain 'F' word, as well. Peter rolled his eyes. The rest of us (except Malcolm) exchanged surreptitious glances, then looked away and left Jesse to wallow in his big, black sulk. Only Malcolm didn't take the hint. He kept asking questions, to which Jesse gave short, gruff answers until a particularly stupid query about handcuffs finally drove him to request, in menacing tones, that Malcolm either shut up or get lost.

Malcolm shut up.

From then on, everyone talked and ate and played games and tried to ignore Jesse, who sat emitting the sort of dark, unhappy vibes that make you uncomfortable. It was as if we were all parked near a pile of rotten garbage, which smelled bad but which couldn't be moved. I think I was more unnerved than anybody. The others just didn't understand his mood, and didn't like it. They hadn't been there at the top of the mineshaft, listening to him wail and plead. They hadn't heard the fear in his voice.

I had. I knew that he was shaken up, and I also knew why. The trouble was, I didn't want to remember any of it. So I tried to forget that he was on the bus, though it wasn't easy. Before, I had found it hard to ignore him because he was like a magnet to me – I couldn't help looking at his face. Now he was just a big, bad reminder of something nasty. I couldn't entirely forget him, any more than I could forget the dentist's appointment written up on Mum's calendar.

Isn't it odd, the way your feelings change? For a while Jesse dazzled me; he seemed to sparkle like a diamond. The next moment, his magical glow had faded. Did it really happen? Did the Abel Harrow business change him, do you think? Or did it change *me*? Did I stop liking Jesse because he had lost his special shine, or did he lose his special shine because I had stopped liking him?

I'm still not sure. On the one hand, Jesse's unusual black mood lasted for several days after our return from Hill End, despite the fact that Tony wasn't in danger. (He had a broken leg and fractured ribs, but was back at school within a month – or was it six weeks? Anyway, whatever it was, he hadn't suffered any permanent damage.) On the other hand, Jesse's miserable period was followed by a reckless one, during which he spread vegemite on the seats of the boys' toilets, smoked cigarettes within sight of the library windows, and did all kinds of disgusting things with chewing gum. In other words, he returned to normal, much to the disappointment of Mrs Patel – who's still teaching our class, by the way, so she can't have got into too much trouble for losing a couple of students. What's more, Jesse didn't stop being friends with Malcolm or Tony. You might have expected that he'd learned his lesson about them, but he hadn't; he was still putting up with their dumb questions and their pointless jokes and their big mouths. To look at them together now, you'd think that the mineshaft episode had never happened.

Except that Jesse seems to be as keen to avoid me as I am to avoid him. Maybe I remind him of Hill End in a way that Tony doesn't. Tony didn't hear him, you see. Tony didn't hear the terror in his voice.

So that's the situation. I don't like Jesse any more. And speaking of not liking a person any more, I'm sorry to say that Mum was right about Richard and Delora. They've split up. It happened not long after their Hill End trip; I just hope that the trip didn't have anything to do with it. I'd feel bad if it did, even though I wasn't the one who encouraged them to go. It was Mum's idea that they should stay in that awful house, without a fridge or electric lights or an indoor toilet. Maybe they argued about it afterwards. I wouldn't be surprised, especially since the whole visit was a total waste of time and effort. I mean, with Eustace turning out to be a hoax, and everything. You might argue that Abel Harrow made up for Eustace, but I don't think Richard or Delora are really convinced about Abel.

Delora said afterwards that she often gets a strong sense of not being wanted in places like Aboriginal sacred sites and wildlife sanctuaries – it's not unusual, apparently. Richard said that the anomaly he picked up on his electromagnetic field detector was 'inconclusive'. Peter can't remember if he got frightened before or after Delora screamed. Only Michelle continues to insist that she was pushed, though Richard seems to believe that she might have tripped over her own feet when Delora panicked.

I know what I think. I think that Abel Harrow has been haunting Golden Gully. He must be a ghost, because the police haven't found him yet. Samantha says that they searched the gully and its surroundings three or four times, after Jesse and Tony fell down that mineshaft, without success. There wasn't a trace of Abel: no tent, no hut, no footprints, no nothing – only a burnt-out camp-fire that could have been lit by anyone. According to Samantha, the police are now keeping an 'eye open' for Abel. Hill End's inhabitants have been told to report his whereabouts if he's ever spotted, even though most of them seem to think that he's disappeared into the hills for a while – maybe wandered off to another, more remote, fossicking area around Sofala, or something.

Michelle and I think differently. We think that he might have found Michelle's bracelet. Why not? He's disappeared. He's left no trace. Maybe we've got rid of him – driven his spirit back to the spirit world, the way Eglantine's was driven back. I certainly hope so, because Michelle really *was* busted when she got home. Her mum won't let her wear proper jewellery any more, not the stuff made of gold and silver. Just fake stuff, which Michelle won't wear. I feel a bit bad about that. Michelle's jewellery has always been very important to her. If Abel's spirit has been laid to rest, however, she won't have made her sacrifice in vain.

And even if it hasn't been laid to rest – even if he shows up again – I'm still sure that he's a ghost. How could I not be, after what Samantha found out from the family history records at the Hill End Museum and Visitor Centre? Richard and Delora never visited the museum, you see. Delora was too 'drained', after the Golden Gully incident, to do anything but go straight back to Sydney. So I had to ask Samantha if she would check the museum for any information on the Harrow clan. Perhaps Abel Harrow might be a relative of Evie and Eustace; could she find out, please? If it wasn't too much trouble.

I wasn't expecting much, to be honest. I thought Samantha would say 'yes, yes' and forget about the whole thing. But I was wrong. She went up to the museum one day and discovered that it contained a whole room full of family history records. When she checked these records, she uncovered the fact that there had been at least one miner called Abel Harrow (died 1889), but that no one else in the Harrow family tree had been named after him. Evie's husband's name had been Claude James. Her brothers' names had been Cyril George, Albert Edward and Thomas Lynton. Her nephews had been called Bernard, Philip and Thomas, her cousins Ernest and William, her sons Gilbert and Eustace. There wasn't another 'Abel' to be seen.

'It's very odd,' Samantha wrote to me, 'because you'd think that two people called Harrow would be part of the same family, wouldn't you? Especially when they've been living in the same area. It's not really a common name. I have to say I was convinced that Abel must be Evie's brother or cousin, but there's no trace of him in the family tree. So I don't know. Maybe there's another branch not mentioned in the files. That's certainly what Karen Smythe thinks. She's the NPWS officer who's been helping me, and she says a lot of their records are incomplete. She also says that the Abel Harrow who hangs around Golden Gully might not be named Abel Harrow at all. People have been calling him that for years, but she doesn't know why – because as far as she's aware, no one in town has ever talked to him. So perhaps there's been a misunderstanding, and only one Abel Harrow has ever existed. He was Eustace's great-great-uncle, by the way – Evie's father-in-law's uncle. According to Alf, he died in a mining accident before Evie's husband's father was even born.

'Oh – did I tell you that we're on good terms with Alf, now? I was so sad to hear about what he'd done for Evie that I couldn't stay angry with him for long, poor man. I mean it's pitiful, really, when you think about it. So I'm making a little grotto in the garden called "Evie's grotto", which I'm filling with her favourite flowers, and a sculpture of a little boy, and a plaque embedded with glass (representing water), pebbles (representing earth), burned wood (representing fire) and hollow pockets (representing air). I told Alf he was welcome to come over any time and sit there, so he could meditate on Evie's memory. He hasn't, so far — at least, he says he hasn't. But I found a funny little pile of nutshells and bottle tops there the other day, so even though he insists he hasn't "set foot on our property" since Richard surprised him, that night, he must have.

'Mustn't he?

'By the way, I have to tell you about the odd thing that happened when I was up at the museum, the other evening. I thought it might interest you because of your haunted house experience. Karen was letting me use the little records room after hours, since I was still chasing down Abel Harrow, and I thought I was alone in the building. But then I heard boards creaking! Well — you can imagine how alarmed I was. I went to see who was walking around in the hallway, and there was no one there. There was no one in any of the rooms, either. But when I went into the Hospital Room, it was freezing cold, as if an airconditioner was running, even though the rest of the place was stinking hot. When I told Karen about this afterwards, she said I must have run into Granny Evans, the hospital ghost!

'Of course, after our experience with "Eustace" I am very sceptical about so-called ghosts, but I must admit it was very creepy . . .'

Interesting, eh?

I told Peter and Michelle about this letter, and they reacted quite differently. Michelle got all excited, and tried to make her mother promise that they would go to Hill End during the school holidays, even though the chances of *that* happening are pretty slim;

Michelle's mum prefers beach holidays. Peter was more sceptical. He's still undecided about Abel, let alone Granny Evans, and pointed out that creaking boards and cold draughts aren't unusual in old houses. I suppose he's hard to convince because he never had anything to do with Eglantine – he just hasn't developed a nose for the supernatural, the way I have. He doesn't know the signs. But he remains open-minded, and keen to hear about anything else that I might dig up on the subject of paranormal apparitions.

As a matter of fact – and I know you won't believe this, I know you'll think I'm fooling myself (don't laugh, please, I realise how ridiculous it sounds) – but as a matter of fact, I think – I *think* – that Peter Cresciani might have a little, tiny bit of a crush on me. Just a little one. Of course, I might be wrong. I probably am. Maybe it's just the ghosts that he's interested in, and that's why he follows me around all the time. He's *certainly* interested in Eglantine. He keeps asking about her, and about my house, and about Bethan, and about the PRISM people. To be honest, he's quite a good person to talk to. Funny, you know? Intelligent. Enthusiastic. Not like Jesse Gerangelos.

Isn't it odd how you can put so much energy into a fake, when all the while there's something much, much more promising practically staring you in the face?

At least I know enough, now, not to make the same mistake in the future.